WILDERS OF WYATT COUNTY:
Their hearts are as big as the
wide-open Wyoming sky.

♥ ♥ ♥

Ace Wilder had always seemed so sure
of himself.

But now he looked as though he needed someone to
cradle and comfort him, and Belinda wished with
all her heart that someone was she.

"Belinda, I..."

"Shh." She pressed her fingertips to his lips, stilling
whatever it was Ace had been about to say. Then
she slipped her arms around his waist and rested her
head against his shoulder. "Don't say anything."

He didn't. Ace wrapped his arms around her
shoulders and rested his cheek against the top of her
head. His breath came out in a long, quiet sigh. It
wasn't the sigh so much as the quiet, trusting way
he rested his cheek against her head that tore a hole
through Belinda's heart and left it gaping.

The truth rushed out and swamped her. She was in
love with Ace!

Dear Reader,

This September, you may find yourself caught up in the hustle and bustle of a new school year. But as a sensational stress buster, we have an enticing fall lineup for you to pamper yourself with. Each month, we offer six brand-new romances about people just like you—trying to find the perfect balance between life, career, family and love.

For starters, check out *Their Other Mother* by Janis Reams Hudson—a feisty THAT SPECIAL WOMAN! butts head with a gorgeous, ornery father of three. This also marks the debut of this author's engaging new miniseries, WILDERS OF WYATT COUNTY.

Sherryl Woods continues her popular series AND BABY MAKES THREE: THE NEXT GENERATION with an entertaining story about a rodeo champ who becomes victi to his matchmaking daughter in *Suddenly, Annie's Father*. And for those of you who treasure stories about best-friends-turned-lovers, don't miss *That First Special Kiss* by Gina Wilkins, book two in her FAMILY FOUND: SONS AND DAUGHTERS series.

In *Celebrate the Child* by Amy Frazier, a military man becomes an integral part of his precious little girl's life—as well as that of her sweet-natured adopted mom. And when a secret agent takes on the role of daddy, he discovers the family of his dreams in Jane Toombs's *Designated Daddy*. Finally, watch for *A Cowboy's Code* by talented newcomer Alaina Starr, who spins a compelling love story set in the hard-driving West.

I hope you enjoy these six emotional romances created *by* women like you, *for* women like you!

Sincerely,

Karen Taylor Richman
Senior Editor

Please address questions and book requests to:
Silhouette Reader Service
U.S.: 3010 Walden Ave., P.O. Box 1325, Buffalo, NY 14269
Canadian: P.O. Box 609, Fort Erie, Ont. L2A 5X3

JANIS REAMS HUDSON

THEIR OTHER MOTHER

Silhouette®

SPECIAL ▼ EDITION®

Published by Silhouette Books
America's Publisher of Contemporary Romance

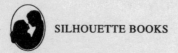 **SILHOUETTE BOOKS**

ISBN 0-373-24267-0

THEIR OTHER MOTHER

Copyright © 1999 by Janis Reams Hudson

This edition published by arrangement with Harlequin Books S.A.

® and TM are trademarks of Harlequin Books S.A., used under license.
Trademarks indicated with ® are registered in the United States Patent
and Trademark Office, the Canadian Trade Marks Office and in other
countries.

Visit us at www.romance.net

Printed in U.S.A.

JANIS REAMS HUDSON

was born in California, grew up in Colorado, lived in Texas for a few years and now calls central Oklahoma home. She is the author of more than twenty-five novels, both contemporary and historical romances. Her books have appeared on the Waldenbooks, B. Dalton and Bookrack bestseller lists and earned numerous awards, including the National Readers' Choice Award and Reviewers' Choice awards from *Romantic Times Magazine*. She is a three-time finalist for the coveted RITA Award from Romance Writers of America and is a past president of RWA.

The Wilders and the Randalls

WILDERS OF WYATT COUNTY—
Their hearts are as big as the wide-open Wyoming sky

The Wilders:

Melissa Garrett (d)
 *
 * ------------------ Jack
 *
King Wilder (d)
 ||
 ||
Betty Anderson (d)

- Rachel
- Trey
- Ace
  ||
  ||
  - Jason
  - Clayton
  - Grant

Cathy Randall (d)

The Randalls:

Howie Randall
 ||
 ||
Elaine Smith

- Belinda

====== denotes marriage
------ denotes illegitimate children
* denotes liaison outside of marriage
(d) means deceased

Chapter One

Ace Wilder heard tires crunching on gravel outside the back door and wondered who would be pulling up to the house. Most people knew enough to park at the barn or the stables if they wanted somebody in the middle of the day.

Ace carried his sandwich to the back door to look out. Eating on the move with his entire meal in one hand had become a fact of life lately around the Flying Ace Ranch. Things had gone to hell in a handbasket since Aunt Mary left. Maybe when Elaine got here later in the week things would smooth out some. His mother-in-law was a born caretaker. Just like Cathy had been.

The pain had eased during the past two years. He could think of his late wife now without feeling like his insides were being ripped out. He had even learned to say the phrase, "Cathy is dead," without flinching.

Cathy's mother was coming to take care of the boys while Ace looked around for a housekeeper to handle everything Aunt Mary used to do. Not that Ace had the slightest idea where he would find such a person in Wyatt County, Wyoming. Every woman he knew—at least the ones he would trust with his sons—had her own house to keep, her own children to raise or had already done those things and was too old to want to do them again for someone else.

It was a good thing Elaine was planning on staying the whole summer. Ace had a feeling it was going to take him at least that long to find someone who could handle his three little hellions, without bloodshed or permanent psychological damage on either side.

Someone who could cook, he thought, taking another bite of his stale sandwich.

Thinking more about his stomach than about why someone would be pulling up at the back of the house, Ace nudged open the screen door with his shoulder and stepped onto the back porch.

It wasn't the fancy red sports car with Colorado tags that had every muscle in his body suddenly tightening in protest, it was the woman climbing out of it. Ye gods and little fishes. The Wicked Witch of the West—in the flesh. Nice flesh, he admitted. But then, he'd been told that a porcupine had nice flesh, too, underneath all those quills.

Just the sight of this woman tightened his gut and made him groan.

Belinda Randall was as sleek and long-legged as any woman had a right to be, and then some, but he wouldn't say she was restful on the eyes. There was nothing restful about her. Her short black hair might be ordinary enough, but the sun struck fiery streaks through it that spoke of heat, of sheer energy. Her gray eyes were as changeable as the weather, dark as thunderheads one minute, soft as morning fog the next. And that lower lip of hers could smile or pout in the blink of an eye. She was all perpetual motion, restless energy, fire. And, Cathy's sister or not, she was a royal pain in the backside.

"Tell me you're lost," he said to her, making every effort to keep from grinding his teeth. "Please, tell me you're lost."

"In your dreams, Wilder." She shook her head slowly and smirked. "I'm here on purpose."

Ace let out a breath. "A nightmare, then."

"You got that right." She slammed the car door and propped her hands on her hips. "*My* nightmare."

Ace leaned against the porch post. "You're too late. We finished castrating last week. But then, we only castrate calves around here, anyway, so maybe you wouldn't have enjoyed it."

She gave one sharp nod of her head. "The war's still on, then. Battle lines drawn. Suits me just fine, cowboy—"

"That's 'rancher' to you."

"—but you might get tired of it before I do. I'm here for the duration."

"What duration?" With a whole new regard for how the passengers on the *Titanic* must have felt upon being told the ship was sinking, Ace straightened away from the porch post. "Why are you here?"

Oh, she did enjoy that wary look on his face, Belinda decided. If she had to put herself in his vicinity for the next several weeks, she wanted him just as miserable and irritated as she was.

She was already over that first hard jolt that struck her each time she saw him again on one of her infrequent visits to this big, empty corner of the world. She didn't like that nasty jolt, didn't like him, but both were facts of life.

No man should be allowed to look like Ace Wilder. No face that rugged should be considered handsome. He had a slight bump on the bridge of his nose, deep grooves bracketing a mouth that was usually set in a hard, unforgiving line, white lines fanning out from the corners of his eyes, with a crescent-shaped scar beside the right one. But handsome he was. Breathtakingly so. She'd always wondered why that fact irritated her so much.

Belinda could easily imagine her younger sister taking one look at this six-foot package of lean male muscle, with those Wilder blue eyes and coal-black hair just long enough to intrigue, and tumbling headfirst into love with him. Which was exactly what Cathy had done.

Cathy had been naive that way.

Belinda wasn't. She didn't like Ace Wilder, not one little bit. No man should be that cocksure of himself. But she was here, and there was no getting around it.

"I'm here because my mother blackmailed me, and I'm here for the summer or until you hire someone to take care of my nephews, whichever comes first."

Ace eyed her like a man eyeing a rattler coiled to strike. "The hell you say. Where's Elaine?"

A wild whoop from the corner of the house cut off her answer. "Aunt Binda! Hey, guys, it's Aunt Binda!"

Belinda turned and braced herself just in time to keep from being knocked flat by the high-speed impact of four sturdy young bodies—three boys and a scruffy yellow mutt the size of a small sofa. They were loud, they were dirty, and they smelled suspiciously like something a person should scrape off the bottom of a shoe before stepping indoors. And Belinda loved them so much—the boys, at least, the verdict was still out on the dog—that she ached with it. They were the sweetest, dearest beings on earth. Despite the elbows and knees jabbing her more-tender places, she hugged them close.

"Oh, my." With a huge grin, she stared down at the three most adorable faces on the planet. Adorable despite being the spitting image of their father, whom she utterly detested. "Who are you guys? What have you done with my nephews?"

"Aw, Aunt Binda." Jason, the oldest at six, grinned and socked her in the arm.

"Jason," Ace said tersely. "What's the rule?"

"Uh-oh." Four-year-old Clay grinned at Jason.

"Aw, Dad," Jason whined. "It was just a little one."

"What's the rule?" Ace repeated.

Jason heaved a sigh. "Boys don't hit girls."

"What's the rest of it?" Ace demanded quietly.

Jason sighed again. "Ever. Boys don't hit girls, ever. I'm sorry, Aunt Binda. I forgot. I didn't mean to hit you."

Belinda wanted to protest. It had been just a friendly tap on the arm from a six-year-old, for heaven's sake. It wasn't as if he'd tried to hurt her. But the look on Ace's face made her think better of interfering with the way he disciplined his own children. It really wasn't her place to criticize. At least not yet, and not in front of the boys.

"Apology accepted," she told Jason. Then she grinned again. "But I'd still like to know what you've done with my nephews. Where are they?"

"Aw, gee," Jason said, his good humor restored. "You know it's us."

"Nope." Belinda shook her head. "You look like Jason, but you're too big."

"I grew!"

"It's really us, Aunt Binda." Clay jumped up and down on Belinda's toes. "Honest!"

Belinda squinted down at him. "Oh, yeah? Well, then, you must be Clayton. But who's this fellow?" She hoisted two-year-old Grant onto her hip. Surely a two-year-old wouldn't notice that her hands were suddenly shaking. He was the child who shouldn't have been. The child her sister gave her life for. Because of that, maybe Belinda loved him just a little bit extra.

Oh, how he'd grown! She'd seen him a mere six months ago, but he'd changed so much. They all had. Her throat tightened with emotion at how much of his life—of all their lives—she had missed.

"That's Grant," Jason said, laughing.

"He was just a baby last time you saw us," Clay told her.

The boy on her hip nodded. "I Grant. I used to be a baby, but I's big now."

"You sure are," Belinda told him.

"Did you come to stay with us?" Jason asked. "Did Grandma come with you?"

"Yes," Belinda said, "and no."

"Huh?"

Belinda laughed. "Yes, I came to stay with you, but no, Grandma didn't come with me. She got sick and couldn't come, but she sends her love."

Jason looked up at her with a sober expression. "Did she die, like our mother?"

That fast, Belinda's eyes stung. A giant fist squeezed her heart. "Oh, no, honey." She dropped to her knees and hugged him, then pulled all three boys into her embrace. "No, Grandma didn't die. She just got a nasty ol' case of pneumonia, that's all. The doctors gave her medicine and she's getting all better. She just has to stay home and rest, and pretty soon she'll be as good as new, I promise."

"Can we send her a get-well card?" Clay asked cheerfully.

Leave it to Clay. Nothing could squash his spirit for long. "She would like that very much."

"Will you help us make it?" Jason, too, was now smiling again.

"You betcha," Belinda told him. "We can even e-mail her some virtual flowers."

The boys' eyes rounded.

"Grandma's got e-mail?" Jason breathed. "Really?"

"Really."

"What's virgil fowlers?" Clay wanted to know.

Belinda chuckled. "It's virtual flowers, and I'll show you later."

Ace sauntered over and stood beside them. It irritated Belinda to no end that he couldn't just walk, like a normal man. He sauntered. There was no other word to describe that slow, deliberate, long-legged movement that probably sent the hearts of weak-willed women—which Belinda definitely was not—

fluttering all over Wyoming. No other word but *saunter.* Unless it was mosey. Or maybe strut.

"Okay, boys," he said to his sons. "Weren't you going to clean out the chicken house today?"

"Aw, Dad." Clay grinned. Clay grinned at everything.

Jason's eyes twinkled, but his smile barely curved his lips. "Aw, Dad."

"Aw, Dad," Grant mimicked.

"Go on, now, so I can talk to Aunt Belinda. And try to make it back to the house with a few eggs this time, will ya?" Ace ruffled the hair on the two tallest boys and winked at Grant.

"We always make it back with eggs," Jason protested. "Lots of eggs."

"And most of them are broken by the time you get them to the house," Ace reminded. "They're food, not ammunition."

"Aw, Dad," Jason said, his grin spreading wider. "You take all the fun out of everything."

"I'll take all the fun out of you," Ace said in a mock threat.

With a shriek of giggles, all three boys unlatched themselves from Belinda's legs and dashed out of sight around the corner of the house, the dog barking excitedly as he raced after them.

Ace watched them go, his gaze lingering until they disappeared. The instant they were out of earshot, he folded his arms across his chest and turned back to Belinda. "Elaine was fine when I talked to her last week."

"She wasn't fine. She's been sick for weeks and lying to all of us because she wanted to come here and spend the summer with her grandsons." Belinda stopped, then frowned. "Don't you think the boys are a little young to be taking on ranch chores?"

Ace counted slowly to ten. Then he started over and did it again before he trusted himself to speak. "No, I don't think they're too young to have what amounts to an Easter egg hunt every day. And that's the last time I ever want to hear you question how I raise my sons. What do you mean she's been sick for weeks?"

"Just what I said. Do you have hay in your ears?"

"To blazes with this."

"Manure, more likely."

"If I want a straight answer, I guess I'll have to call her myself." He turned to go, aiming to get away from this woman who had the rare ability to make him tense, irritable, and downright angry. He was usually none of those things. Only with Belinda.

Long, elegant fingers with short, unpolished nails latched on to his wrist like a steel handcuff. "Don't you dare call her. She needs her rest. She just got out of the hospital yesterday."

Ace stopped and eyed his sister-in-law over his shoulder. "She really had pneumonia?"

"Yes." She didn't so much let go of his arm as toss it away. "She kept saying it was just a cold, that she'd be over it before she came up here. She must have known it was worse than that, because she wouldn't even agree to see a doctor until I promised her I would come up here and take care of the boys if she wasn't able."

Ace had no choice but to believe her. Belinda might be more prickly than a cactus, but she didn't lie. And Elaine loved her grandsons like there was no tomorrow. If she could have been here, she would have been.

Aside from that, Belinda hated his guts. She wouldn't have come to the ranch—especially not planning to stay the whole summer—if she didn't have to. "How long is she going to be laid up?"

Belinda's eyes narrowed to slate-gray slits. "If by that you mean when is she coming to take over from me, forget it, buckaroo. She's so run-down it will take her weeks if not months to fully recover. You and I are stuck with each other, Wilder. Get used to it."

"That'll be the day." She'd been on the Flying Ace for all of fifteen minutes, and already his jaw ached from grinding his teeth, and his stomach was eating a hole in itself. He would be out of his mind by this time tomorrow. If she was still here next week, one of them would probably end up dead or legally insane. The woman was a menace.

Since Ace couldn't figure out a way to get her to leave that didn't involve bloodshed—probably his— he strode over to her little toy car and hauled two suitcases out of the tiny back seat. "Might as well get you settled, since you're here."

"Why, thank you for that warm welcome." Belinda batted her eyes at him, then reached in to her passenger seat.

When she straightened beside him, Ace shook his head. "Two purses?"

"One purse, one computer."

Ace shuddered. "Your computer, if I recall—and I do—consists of at least four big boxes of equipment, miles of cables, and blown fuses every other hour."

"That was before they made laptops that weigh less than three pounds." She swung one of the purses under his nose by one finger. "Your fuses are safe. And so," she added with a smirk as she remembered his complaints the last time, "is your poor aching back. No boxes to lug." With a wave of her arm, she motioned toward the house. "Lead the way, cowboy."

Rolling his eyes and flexing his jaw, he did.

Belinda followed the Sauntering Buckaroo to the back door. As slow as he walked, they'd be at this all night. She wondered irritably if he moved that slowly in bed.

The laugh brought on by that errant thought bordered on the hysterical.

Ace stopped and frowned at her. "Something funny?"

"Everything, Wilder." She refused to look at him. "Just every little thing."

"We'll see how funny you think everything is by the time you get supper on the table tonight."

"What, you think I can't cook?"

"Just wondering if you understand that laundry, housecleaning, and cooking are part of the deal. A good, hot meal on the table at six o'clock sharp for a bunch of hungry men and three little boys, and you, if you want to eat with us. Breakfast at 5:00 a.m., and plenty of it, with lunch at noon. Seven days a week."

"Do you have an ad in the paper yet to find a new housekeeper?"

"Tired of your job already?"

"You wish. I can handle the job, Wilder. Maybe not the way Cathy did, or Mary, but I can handle it."

He smirked.

She smirked right back at him. "I'll need to hook my modem to a phone line. I'm not letting my business suffer because you can't keep a woman in your house.''

Those Wilder blue eyes turned to ice.

Belinda admitted she may have crossed the line with that remark about a woman. Her stomach knotted as her own words echoed cruelly in her mind.

''There's a phone jack in your bedroom,'' he said curtly. ''You call long distance, you pay for it.''

Shaking off her discomfort, she refused to dignify his petty comment with a reply. When he held the door open for her, she sailed into the house. She deliberately ignored the bedroom off the kitchen and headed up the stairs to the guest room she normally used when she visited. The downstairs room had been Mary's. Belinda assumed it would be used by the new housekeeper, but she wasn't sleeping that close to the kitchen to save her soul. She would see enough of the kitchen as it was. She sure didn't plan to sleep next to it.

''One more thing,'' Ace told her when they went back out to her car for another load.

She arched a brow. ''Only one?''

His eyes narrowed to sharp slits. ''I know you and I have never had much use for each other—''

''Now there's an understatement.''

''—but I won't have my boys exposed to your hostility toward me.''

''*My* hostility toward *you?*''

''That's right.''

''Oh, and you're so fond of me, right?''

''You're their aunt. I'm their father. For their sake, we don't hammer at each other in front of them.''

''You think you have to tell me how to act around my own nephews?''

"No," he said, surprising her. "I just wanted it said, for the record, so we know where we stand with each other."

"We don't stand anywhere with each other. I stand with and for my sister's children. If you think for a minute I'd do anything to hurt them—"

"I wouldn't have let you out of your car if I did."

Belinda looked at Ace and smiled. "Are you sure you want me to cook for you? Poison is so easy to disguise."

Ace glanced down at his watch. "Hmm. Twenty-seven minutes."

"He can tell time," she observed, reaching into her car for her portable printer.

"That's how long it took you to threaten my life." His lips twitched. "You're slipping, Slim. You usually get that over with in the first ten minutes."

"I promised my mother I'd try to be nice to you."

"So much for keeping your word," he mumbled.

Pulling her printer out of the car, Belinda tossed her head. "You can question my ability, but not my integrity. I promised to try, and I *did* try."

Neither spoke again until the last of her bags was in her room upstairs. Then she told him she'd be downstairs in thirty minutes and shut the door in his face.

She'd done it, Belinda told herself as she leaned her back against the closed door and slid to the floor. She had kept her word to her mother and come to Wyoming as promised, and she'd faced Ace Wilder and lived through the inevitable confrontation. In thirty minutes she would have to do it again.

She had hoped, as she'd pulled up to the house,

that when she saw him those old jittery feelings wouldn't stir to life in her stomach again.

Ridiculous hope. Futile.

All she knew was that somehow, for some reason, she always ended up feeling at a disadvantage around Ace. Vulnerable. Shaky. Threatened?

No, of course not. Men didn't threaten her. She'd been sired and raised by one, married to another—jerk though he turned out to be—and worked with them her entire adult life. She could hold her own with any man.

Which was why her feeling of vulnerability around Ace irritated her so much. She hated it. Hated him for causing it, hated him more for sensing it. The only way she knew to fight that vulnerability, to prove to him and herself that she was not vulnerable, was to strike out.

It was reflex, pure and simple. Habit, now, after all these years. She wasn't proud of it, but there it was. In fact, most of the time she had trouble believing some of the things that came out of her mouth when she was around him.

Dammit, there was just something about Ace Wilder that made her nerves twitch and set her teeth on edge. And she'd let her mother talk her into putting herself in his immediate vicinity for who knew how long.

"Mother, you have no idea what you've done to me."

It was going to be a long, hot summer.

Down at the barn Ace reminded himself yet again to unclench his jaw.

"Problem?"

He turned from staring—glaring, he realized—at the bay mare in the corral to find Jack eyeing him critically.

"That's putting it mildly," Ace admitted. "Elaine came down with pneumonia."

"That's rough. She gonna be okay?"

"She'll be fine. It's the rest of us you better worry about."

"How so?"

"She sent Belinda in her place."

One of Jack's infrequent grins flashed across his face. "No foolin'?"

Ace groaned.

Jack laughed—an even-less-frequent occurrence than his grin. "The boys'll be in hog heaven."

"They already are."

"How long's she staying?"

Trey poked his head out of the barn door. "How long is who staying?"

"Ace's favorite sister-in-law," Jack answered, still grinning.

"The fox?" The youngest Wilder brother threw his head back and let out a howl.

Ace grunted. "I dare you to call her that to her face."

"Oh, no." Trey held his hands out as if to ward off attack. "I'd like to live to see my next birthday."

"Glad to see you're not entirely stupid."

"Of course he's not stupid," Jack said. "He's generally outstanding in his field."

In charge of the Flying Ace crops, Trey didn't even bother to groan at the old pun.

They were a sight, the three Wilder brothers. Tall, lean, muscular and, according to the female population of Wyatt County, good-looking as all get-out. Thick, raven-black hair, strong, angular faces, and eyes as blue as the background for the stars on Old Glory herself.

While their looks were strikingly similar, their personalities were not. Sometimes they clashed, as brothers often did. Ace was the oldest, the ranch operator. When their father, King Wilder, died, he'd left Ace 60 percent of all his worldly goods, and that naturally included the Flying Ace Ranch. King had left the remaining 40 percent to be divided equally among the rest of his children.

There was no jealousy from the other Wilder offspring over that. Jack, Trey, and Rachel were equally grateful not to have been left with the heavy responsibility of running the ranch, making sure it turned enough profit to support them all regardless of falling beef or oil prices, uncooperative weather, and a constant shortage of good help. They all pulled their weight, each having separate responsibilities, but they were satisfied to have Ace hold the position of ranch operator.

Being operator of one of the largest ranches in the state hadn't ever gone to Ace's head as it could have, but he never forgot it, the duty, the responsibility, the past generations looking over his shoulder and judging him. No, he never forgot it. Neither did anyone who had to deal with him.

Jack was the quiet one, but steady as a rock. It was no secret that he was King Wilder's bastard—Ace, Trey, and Rachel's half brother. But to give the devil his due, when King Wilder had learned he had an illegitimate son, he had moved quickly to adopt the boy and change his name to Wilder. Jack had been twelve the day his aunt had dropped him on King's doorstep after the boy's mother had drunk herself to death. There had been more than a few bloody noses among the three brothers in the beginning, but their little sister, Rachel, had calmly and emphatically put a stop to it by declaring that Jack was her brother just as much as Ace and Trey were, and they'd better just stop picking on him. She'd been five at the time, the baby of the family, with every man on the ranch wrapped right around her little-bitty finger. From that moment on, Jack had been accepted.

Trey was the youngest and most outgoing of the three brothers. He'd been twelve when their parents had hit that icy patch that had sent them to their deaths on their way home from Jackson Hole. Ace had been twenty and, in Trey's opinion at the time, had thrown his weight around. He'd made twelve-year-old Trey stay in school, and if that hadn't been bad enough, had packed him off to college right after graduation and made him stay there.

Trey had gotten his degree in agribusiness and floored them all by fixing his attention on crops instead of cattle or horses. Since neither Jack nor Ace was overly fond of the farming aspect of the Flying Ace, they'd stepped back and let Trey have it.

"So how long is Belinda staying?" Trey asked when Ace didn't answer Jack.

Ace grunted. "Until I find a new housekeeper."

Jack was still grinning. "Won't be dull around here, that's for sure."

"I don't know what the hell you're grinning about," Ace said irritably. "She's already threatened to poison me."

"Yeah, but she likes *us*," Trey taunted. "If you

don't have your will made out yet, I want your Winchester.''

"Well now, kid.'' Ace knew how to get a rise out of Trey. He hated being called kid. "I tell you what you do. You wish real hard for that Winchester in one hand, and spit in the other, and see which hand gets filled.''

"Stingy.''

"That's me.''

"I mean, it's not like you can take it with you.''

"Maybe I wanna be buried with it.''

At the shotgun sound of the back screen door whacking shut, the three brothers turned to look toward the house and the woman marching toward them.

"Looks like you might get your chance sooner than you thought,'' Trey said with a snicker.

"What'd you ever do to her, anyway?'' Jack asked.

"Near as I can tell,'' Ace muttered, "I was born.''

One of these days, Ace thought, he was going to take her down and sit on her until she told him once and for all why she hated his guts. From the night they met, at his and Cathy's wedding rehearsal, Belinda had been on the attack. Only when Cathy had been within earshot had Belinda ever held her tongue around him. One of these days...

But first, he figured he was going to have to deal with whatever had put this latest look of irritation on her face.

"Hey, darlin','' Trey called.

"Don't waste your breath, little brother,'' she tossed back. But it was a good-natured toss. The irritation had faded from her face the instant she took her gaze off Ace.

Trey let out an exaggerated sigh and slapped his hand over his heart. "She loves me. You can just tell."

"Of course I do." She grabbed him by the ears and planted a quick, smacking kiss on his mouth. "Like a boil on the backside."

"Welcome back," Jack told her.

Here, Belinda had always thought, was a kindred spirit, of sorts. Because of an accident of birth, Jack had not always been accepted. Their circumstances were different, his and hers, but she recognized that guarded look in his eyes.

"Thanks, Jack," she said, shaking his hand.

"Is there a problem?" Ace asked her.

"No problem." She turned and faced him. "Only that there doesn't seem to be much food in the house, and you neglected to define the word 'bunch' when you told me how many I'd be cooking for."

Trey thumped his hand against his heart again. "And she cooks, too."

Belinda squinted up at Ace. "Did he get dropped on his head when he was a baby?"

Ace pursed his lips to keep from smiling. He wasn't about to let her get a smile out of him. Not that easily. "A time or two," he answered.

She nodded as though weighing some serious matter. "That would explain it, then. Now, about that bunch."

"The three of us, plus three hands, the boys, and you."

"Enough food for ten, then."

Trey winked at her. "We're hungry, darlin'. Make it enough for twenty. That ought to hold us till breakfast. Unless *you* want to hold me till breakfast,'' he added with a goofy leer.

"In your dreams, Number Three."

"Great dreams. Wanna hear about 'em?"

"Not unless you're aiming at becoming my next ex-husband."

Jack hooted with laughter.

"Hell, Trey, she just got here," Ace complained. "Do you have to start hitting on her already?"

"Relax, Ace," Belinda said with a smirk. "If I ever took him up on it, he'd run for his life. And speaking of running, I guess I'll have to make a run into town for groceries. I'll take the boys with me."

"Sorry." Ace grimaced. "Just sign your name on the Flying Ace charge card at Biddle's on Main. I wasn't expecting you—or rather, Elaine—until the end of the week."

"You weren't going to eat?"

"We were making do. Take the Blazer," he added, pointing toward the barn and the white Chevy Blazer parked beside it with the red-and-black Flying Ace logo on the door. "The keys are in it."

"And don't forget," Trey said with a wink. "We're hungry."

Ace eyed her critically. "You do know how to cook, don't you?"

Belinda pursed her lips and narrowed her eyes. "As long as you don't expect me to churn butter or kill and skin my own meat."

Ace hooked his thumbs in the front pockets of his jeans. "Well, there's the chickens, but you don't have to skin 'em. Just pluck 'em. And I wouldn't want you to go to all that trouble your first night here."

She gave him a tight smile. "I'll fix you a meal you won't forget for a long, long time."

"Now that," Ace muttered as she walked away, "is a scary thought."

As soon as Belinda got the boys cleaned up from their romp through the chicken house, she took the list she'd made while they had a water fight in the bathroom and marched them out to the Blazer.

You do know how to cook, don't you?

She'd get him for that. She'd promised him a meal he wouldn't forget, and that's exactly what she'd give him.

"Boys?" she asked as the Blazer shot up a rooster tail of dust behind it while eating up the miles to town. "If you could have anything you wanted for supper tonight, what would it be?"

Three young voices clamored to be heard over each other.

Belinda grinned to herself. Her nephews were going to be thrilled, but Ace Wilder had good reason to worry about his supper.

Chapter Two

Ace was more than wary when he and the men went in for supper. And, as it turned out, with good reason.

"Well," he said, looking over the food on the table. "You didn't have to skin it."

"Clay picked the corn dogs," Jason announced proudly as everyone sat down at the table. "I picked the SpaghettiOs. Grant picked the broccoli." He made a face. "Yuck."

At least, Ace thought with an inward groan, there was plenty of everything.

"Yes sirree." Trey winked at Belinda. "The lady keeps her word. It's darn sure a meal we won't be forgetting for a while."

Belinda smiled and batted her eyes. "I hope so. I hope you particularly remember it the next time you start to ask me a stupid question."

"Oh-ho." Jerry Sutter shot a glance around the table. His amused gaze lit on Trey. "One of you boys pi— uh, hack the lady off?"

"Not me." Trey raised his hands in innocence. "She loves me."

"In your dreams, Number Three." Belinda looked back at Sutter.

"Belinda Randall," Ace said, "meet Jerry Sutter."

"Pleased to meet you," she offered.

With a twist of his head and a wide smile, Sutter said, "The pleasure's all mine, ma'am."

"Jerry signed on about six months ago," Ace added. "Jerry, my sister-in-law, the boys' aunt. She's in charge of the house until I find a new housekeeper."

"Is Aunt Binda in charge of us, too?" Jason asked.

"That's right, squirt," Belinda said. "So eat your broccoli."

She cocked her head and studied this newest hand. He was the youngest of the men at the table, in his mid-twenties, she guessed. About five-nine, with sandy-brown hair cut military short and a curving mustache several shades darker. Brown eyes with a definite twinkle to them.

Sutter's smile stretched wide. "Aunt Binda can be in charge of me anytime."

"Why?" she asked him. "You need somebody to scrub behind your ears and teach you manners?"

Male laughter burst loose like a sudden clap of thunder. Even Sutter laughed, shaking his head.

Still chuckling, Stoney Hamilton grabbed two corn dogs and served himself up a hefty portion of SpaghettiOs. "She got you good, Jerry, she surely did." He winked a wrinkled eye at Ace. "Got you, too, if you're the one who questioned her cooking."

"All I did was ask if she could cook," Ace protested.

Belinda narrowed her eyes at the boss. "Yeah, Slick, but it was the way you asked."

Stoney laughed again. He had been foreman of the Flying Ace since before Ace was born. When King and Betty Wilder died in that car crash up near Jackson Hole right after Ace's twentieth birthday, it had been Stoney who'd made sure Ace and his brothers and sister learned everything there was to know about ranching.

He was old now, half-crippled up from all the various mishaps and injuries that went with cowboying, but he still had a place on the Flying Ace. He wasn't foreman anymore—Jack had taken over that position years ago. But there was still plenty for him to do around the ranch, plenty still for him to teach King Wilder's offspring.

If anybody asked him—which they didn't, but if they did—he'd probably tell them that aside from those three youngest rascals, not enough people gave Ace Wilder a hard time.

Not that Ace hadn't had it rough, what with losing his daddy and mama when he was just twenty, with two younger brothers and a little sister to raise, not to mention a ranch to run. But he'd handled it, Ace had, handled it all. Then he'd brought home that pretty little Cathy as his bride, and things had looked up even more. Once again there were babies on the Flying Ace, and that had been a good thing.

Then came that last baby, little Grant, and Cathy dyin' like that, while giving birth. There were those who said that it was too much, that Ace Wilder would never recover. But the boy—man—was doing all right, even if he did keep too much to himself these days.

Ace was too well respected and well liked for anybody to want to get in his face, as the youngsters said these days. Ace had earned that respect and liking, no doubt about it. But the way Stoney saw it, having this little slip of a woman get the best of him now and then would do Ace good, yes, it would.

Next to Stoney, Frank Thompson, the Flying Ace's horse trainer, jabbed an elbow against Stoney's shoulder. "You gonna eat all them spaghetti whatcha-ma-call-'ems yourself?"

With a grunt, Stoney passed him the bowl.

"Good to have you back, Miz Belinda," Frank said, loading his plate.

"Thank you, Frank." Belinda smiled.

In his mid-fifties, Frank Thompson stood maybe five-six with his boots on. If his legs weren't so bowed that he looked like he was still straddling a horse, some said he'd be at least six feet tall. They didn't say it to his face, but they said it.

He had dark, weather-beaten skin that was lined far beyond his years, twinkling brown eyes, and a nose with two humps in it. He'd been training Flying Ace horses for more than twenty years.

Belinda had a fondness for Frank, although that hadn't always been the case. During her first visit to the ranch, he had—quite against her will and without much cooperation from her—taught her to ride. Once she'd gotten past the achy muscles and beginner's mistakes, she had learned, thanks to Frank's patience, to enjoy herself.

In addition to Frank, Stoney, and Jerry Sutter, Belinda knew there were other men employed by the

Flying Ace, but she'd never met them. The ranch was divided into sections, the largest of which was controlled and managed directly from headquarters. Then there was the farm, which Trey managed, and three other sections.

These latter were actually ranches within a ranch. One occupied the northeast corner, one the northwest and one the southwest. Each had its own house, barn, corrals, pastures. And its own foreman, who reported directly to Jack, as overall foreman of the Flying Ace. These other foremen had homes on their respective sections, provided for them and their families by the Flying Ace.

But these men rarely ever came to headquarters, so Belinda had never met them.

Across the table from Frank, Jack helped himself to the round little circles of spaghetti. "Everything looks good to me," he said. "But we gotta find something else Grant likes besides broccoli."

Belinda grinned at him. "We were trying to cover most of the major food groups. Or at least the colors," she added, laughing. "We needed something green, and there wasn't enough time for lime Jell-O to set."

"Thank God for small favors," Ace muttered. The thought of lime Jell-O made him shudder. And Belinda's response to Jack made him frown. If *he'd* said that about the broccoli, she would have jumped down his throat. But for Jack, she smiled. Go figure.

But then, it had always seemed to be just him, Ace, who brought out Belinda's prickly side.

No, that wasn't true, Ace admitted. She could be prickly with anybody when she wanted to. It just seemed like she was more prickly with him, more often, than with anybody else. Sometimes, he realized, she reminded him of Jack, back when he'd first come to the Flying Ace.

Come to. That was a joke, a sick one. Jack had been practically shoved out of his aunt's car and left here. Until that minute, no one in the Wilder family, including King Wilder himself, had known Jack even existed. But one look at that face and it was obvious to a blind man that twelve-year-old Jack Garrett was King Wilder's son.

Damn, had it really been twenty years? On the one hand, it seemed like only yesterday that Ace had learned that his father had had a fling twelve years earlier with a barmaid named Melissa Garrett over in Cheyenne. She'd given birth to King Wilder's son and never said a word to him about it. She'd carted her kid from town to town, bar to bar, while she'd taken up with one man after another and proceeded to slowly drink herself to death. She'd finally succeeded in the latter just before her son's twelfth birthday.

Her sister, Linda, had ended up with Jack, and had no desire to keep him. It must have been no secret in her family as to who sired the boy, because she'd driven him straight to the Flying Ace and dumped him on the doorstep. Literally.

At the time, Ace had been so full of anger that he hadn't seen, hadn't cared, what such an experience did to a terrified, vulnerable twelve-year-old. All he'd known was that his father had cheated on his mother, and suddenly he had an extra brother he didn't want.

He remembered that look of nervy defiance in Jack's eyes—eyes the same brilliant blue as his own, as Trey's and Rachel's. As their father's. Ace remembered the chip on those thin, underfed shoulders. The I-don't-care-if-nobody-wants-me jerk of his chin. All covering up a world of hurt.

Yeah, Ace remembered the look, the chip, the attitude, all right. They'd gotten past it, somehow. Mostly because of Rachel, he supposed. She had loved her new brother on sight. She'd been five years old and had ruled the Flying Ace with her dimples and her smile. With an occasional temper tantrum thrown in for effect.

It had been many years now since Ace could even remember what it had been like without Jack. They were brothers, he and Jack and Trey. That said it all, in his book. Brothers.

But every time he saw Belinda Randall he couldn't help but remember that look of Jack's, that chip, that attitude. He saw them plainly in her, and he'd never understood it. She hadn't been abandoned on somebody's doorstep. She wasn't the illegitimate offspring of some stranger. Her mother hadn't drunk herself to death. Hell, the Randalls were a close family, loving, supportive. And Belinda was part of that. Truth to tell, she'd had a better, kinder upbringing than Ace had.

He shook his head. He just didn't understand this woman at all.

"What's Rachel up to this summer?" Belinda asked him.

Mildly surprised by her polite question and civil tone, Ace speared another stalk of broccoli with his fork. "She's working in the university lab this summer."

"What's she got, one more year?"

"Yeah. She'll get her vet license next spring."

"And none too soon," Jack muttered. "We're down to one vet for the whole county. We need her."

The talk around the table turned to animal medical emergencies, then to downed fences, rampaging moose and elk, the wild horse herds that swept through the area. Belinda was so interested in what the men were saying—it was a far cry from her usual conversations about HTML coding, Java and cgi scripts, databases, table layouts, and overall web designs—that she hadn't realized everyone was finished eating until Trey spoke.

"Okay," he said, bracing his hands against the edge of the table. "I'll risk my neck here, or maybe my stomach, and ask, since nobody else seems to be brave enough." He was looking straight at Belinda.

"Ask what?" she asked.

He swallowed with an audible gulp. "Is there any dessert?"

Belinda laughed. "Got ya scared, do I?"

"Yes, ma'am."

"We got dessert, don't we, Aunt Binda?"

"Yes, sir, Mr. Jason, we sure do."

A cautious sigh of relief made its way around the table.

Belinda rose and came back smiling a moment later with a platter from the pantry. "Gentlemen, I give you...dessert."

Silence first. Followed shortly by booming laughter when, with a flourish, she presented two dozen packages of Ding Dongs.

"Who wants ice cream with his chocolate cake?"

While Belinda cleaned up the kitchen and loaded the dishwasher, the boys went outside to play with

Scooter. When she finished, she poked her head out the back door. "Anybody here wanna send an e-mail to Grandma?"

"I do, I do!" came three young voices.

"Well, all right then, let's go."

She led them upstairs to her room.

"That's your computer?" Jason stared wide-eyed at the micronotebook set up on a folding table next to the dresser in Belinda's bedroom. "That little thing?"

"Yes," she said carefully. "You can all look. But here's the deal. This computer is how I earn my living. It's not a toy. You have to promise me, all three of you, that you will never, ever touch it, not any part of it, unless I'm with you. Deal?"

"Deal," they said in unison.

"Okay." But just to be safe, she would keep it on the top closet shelf when she wasn't using it. Lightweight portability had its disadvantages. "Let's get busy," she said. "Grandma needs flowers."

First she logged on to the server in her office back in Denver and set up an e-mail account for the boys. After all, she told them, Grandma would surely want to answer any message they sent her. Then Belinda took them onto the Internet to one of the sites that e-mailed pictures of flower bouquets for free and let the boys choose what to send. They decided on colorful balloons instead of flowers.

Belinda smiled. "Oh, she'll like these."

"You think so?" Jason asked.

"I know so. What should we say on the card?"

"Get well, Grandma?" Jason offered.

"How come you get to say?" Clay demanded.

"How come?" Grant echoed.

"We can all say whatever we want," Belinda told them easily. "Jason wants to say 'Get well, Grandma.' What do you want to say, Clay?"

"I wanted to say the same thing."

"Okay, how about this? We can say 'Get well, Grandma.'" She typed as she spoke.

"Is that what that says?" Clay wanted to know.

"Uh-huh. Then we'll sign Jason's name to it. Then," she got in before Clay could protest, "we'll type in your message, Clay. Do you want to say the same thing?"

By the time they finished, each boy had told Grandma to get well, and their attention was starting to wander.

"When will Grandma get the balloons?" Clay asked.

"As soon as she checks her e-mail. Maybe tonight, maybe tomorrow."

"Ooh, cool. Clowns."

"This is the Kids Channel. Here." She showed Jason how to move his finger over the touch pad to point and click. Since he'd only just finished first grade, she had to read most of the text to him, but he caught on to the graphic links instantly. A few minutes later she had to practically force him to give each of his brothers a turn, but she had a ball introducing them to the wonders of the Internet.

Ace stood at the door to her room and watched. They had their backs to him, so they didn't know he was there. He was glad. He didn't want them to see the confusion running through him just then. He'd meant to teach them himself about the Internet; he'd just never found the time, nor an appropriate method.

And they seemed too young to understand. Or maybe he was too old to explain.

Belinda made explaining cyberspace look easy. He supposed he was grateful to her for introducing them to the technology. He *was* grateful. He just didn't like feeling grateful to her.

When their attention started drifting again, Belinda disconnected from the Internet and shut down her computer. "I'll bet it's bath time."

"Aw, jeez, Aunt Binda," Jason complained.

"Aw, jeez," Grant echoed.

Clay made a face. "We don't need no baf."

"You," she said, narrowing her eyes and poking a finger against Clay's chest, "smell like a dog."

Clay giggled. "So?"

"So," she said, tickling his ribs and making him shriek. "Any critter that smells like a dog has to sleep out in the doghouse and eat dog food out of the dog bowl."

Jason bounced on his toes. "Honest, Aunt Binda? We can sleep in the doghouse?"

Ace leaned his shoulder against the doorjamb and chuckled. "Don't look now, Aunt Binda, but I think you just blew it, big-time."

Belinda gave him a narrow-eyed look. "And I can tell that pleases you, Daddy."

"Not me," he denied with another chuckle. "I just want to see how you get yourself out of this one."

"Can we take the flashlight?" Jason wanted to know.

"Yeah, fash-light," Grant mimicked.

"Flashlight?" With an effort, Belinda tore her gaze from the sight of Ace lounging in her bedroom doorway. "Dogs don't get flashlights. Or pillows or blankets or mattresses."

Since she'd quit tickling Clay, he had stopped giggling. Now his lower lip trembled. "Do we have to sleep with Scooter? I think he gots fleas."

Belinda mashed her lips together to keep from grinning and smoothed a hand over his thick, black hair. "Fleas, huh? Well…I suppose you could sleep in your beds if you took a bath."

"Come on, guys." Clay jumped up and barreled toward the door. "We're gonna take our bath now, Dad."

Chuckling as he turned to follow his sons to the bathroom at the end of the hall, Ace tossed back over his shoulder, "Nice save, Aunt Binda. I'll handle bath time."

Belinda sat where she was, her fists clenched against her thighs. She didn't want him to laugh, didn't want him to be nice to her. It made the jittery feeling in the pit of her stomach, the one that came over her every time she got near him, just that much worse. Made her feel all quaky inside.

She didn't like feeling quaky.

The boys were normally allowed a half hour of television after their bath, before going to bed. Tonight Belinda changed the rules on them and made them help her clean up the bathroom.

"But we're just little kids," Jason protested.

"Little kids," Grant repeated with a sly grin.

"You're water monkeys. A person could drown in the water you guys left on the floor."

In seconds she had them mopping up the floor with their towels, and singing the "Volga Boatmen Song."

"'Yo-ho *heave,* ho.'"

The floor practically got polished, because they didn't want to quit singing. Or giggling.

"I think I've created a monster," she muttered.

"Three of them," Ace said from the doorway.

Belinda jumped. She pressed a hand over her heart to keep it from leaping out of her chest. "I thought you'd gone downstairs."

"Sorry, didn't mean to scare you. I was coming back to clean up the mess." He folded his arms over his chest and looked down at his three grinning sons. "I like this arrangement much better."

There he went again, she thought, being nice to her. She didn't want him being nice. Flustered, she turned away.

"But I have to admit," he added, "that I'm surprised."

She arched a brow in question.

"This? From the woman who thought they were too young to handle chores?"

"Let's just say I've seen the light."

"Good." He nodded. "Now, if you can just get them to make their beds in the mornings..."

She turned away from him. "Okay," she said to the boys. "That's plenty. You can go down and watch TV now. You did a good job."

As fast as she could, she snatched up the wet towels and followed the boys downstairs.

Frowning, Ace watched her go. What the hell had that been about? He'd complimented her handling of the boys, and she couldn't wait to get away from him.

Just as well, he figured. Whenever they stayed in the same room together too long—like more than thirty seconds—all they did was pick at each other. Someday he was going to figure out why.

He went to his room and changed out of his wet shirt. Should have taken it off before the boys' bath.

By the time he got downstairs, Belinda was snuggled in his recliner before the television, and all three boys were sprawled across her.

"Hey, come on, guys," he said. "Aunt Binda's tired. Give her a break, will ya?"

With Clay's feet framing her ears, she frowned up at Ace. "I'm not tired."

Ace found himself wanting to trace the dark circles beneath her eyes, but thought better of it. She'd probably snap his fingers off. He tucked them safely into the front pockets of his jeans. "You look tired."

"Yeah, well, so do you, cowboy."

"Rancher. And I am tired. Any coffee left?"

"Sure," she answered. He was halfway to the kitchen when he heard her mutter, "In the pantry, in the can marked Folgers."

She hadn't said it to amuse him, but to irritate him. He knew that. Still, he found himself clamping his jaw tight to keep from chuckling. He wasn't going to laugh. She wasn't going to make him laugh. Not, at least, until he was in the privacy of his own bedroom with the door shut.

Damn her. How could she be so irritating one minute, and make him want to laugh the next?

He started a fresh pot of coffee and hung around in the kitchen while it brewed. Normally he made it a point to spend this half hour of TV time with the boys. It was their time together, the four of them.

Not that he hadn't been seeing a great deal of them all day, every day, since Mary had left. His brothers and the hands had had to take up the slack while Ace kept a close eye on his sons for the past couple of weeks. As much as he missed Mary, and as desperately as he needed a new housekeeper, he was grateful for those two weeks when there had been only him to care for the boys. He hadn't felt this close to them or spent so much time with any of them since they were each newborns. He was sorry for that, and when he did find a housekeeper, he wasn't going to make the same mistake again of letting someone else make all the decisions regarding his sons.

Cathy had been a good mother, a wonderful mother. If she had kept the boys to herself for the most part, it was because Ace had let her. She had thought that was what he wanted. Maybe he'd thought so, too. But no longer.

They were awfully quiet in there, he thought, but resisted the urge to check on them. Belinda hadn't even seen them in six months. She might just barely tolerate *him,* but there wasn't a doubt in his mind about how much she loved her nephews. He would give her these few minutes alone with them while he waited on the coffee.

The hiss, spit and drizzle of the coffeemaker was the only sound in the kitchen. He'd never realized just how quiet the house could be at night.

Jack had gone back to his own house for the night. When Jack took over as foreman a few years ago, Stoney had insisted on moving out of the foreman's house and into the bunkhouse with the other hands. Jack, Ace knew, had been reluctant to move into the small house at the other end of the complex. He didn't want Stoney to feel as if he were being completely pushed aside. But Stoney had finally convinced him that he didn't like living alone and would prefer the company of the other men in the bunkhouse. Of course, right now the only other man in the bunkhouse was Jerry, since Ace had fired Dan Jenkins last month for drinking on the job.

So Jack lived alone in the foreman's house, and he seemed to like it just fine.

Ace had liked it, too, for a while. It had given him and Cathy more privacy. Especially after Rachel had gone off to college and Trey had built his own house on the north side of the ranch to be near his crops.

Now, with Aunt Mary gone, it was just Ace and the boys. Despite the noise those three active boys could make, the house seemed too…still. Too quiet. Empty.

On the wall beside the refrigerator, the phone rang. When Ace answered, he was pleased to hear his mother-in-law's voice.

"Elaine. How are you feeling?"

"Much better." But her voice was huskier than usual. "Did Belinda get there all right?"

"Early this afternoon."

"I'm so sorry about all of this, Ace."

"You can't help it if you got sick," he protested. "You don't have anything to apologize for."

"I know you and Belinda don't always get along."

Now there was an understatement. "We're bumping along okay." If he didn't count being served corn dogs and canned spaghetti circles for supper, he thought with a rueful grin. "She's great with the boys, Elaine, you know that. That's the important thing."

He heard her let out a heavy sigh. "Can I talk to them? I want to thank them for the balloons."

"What balloons?"

"Oh, what do they call it? Virtual balloons. They sent me a picture of balloons, with their get-well wishes on them, through e-mail. I wanted to thank them."

"So that's what they were up to. Hold on, I'll get them." He put the phone down and went to the living room to get the boys, and stopped short at the sight that greeted him. They were asleep. All of them. Belinda lay back in his big recliner, dozing with all three sleeping boys draped over and across her in various poses.

If anyone ever wanted to know what the human body would be like without bones, they had only to look at a sleeping child. Clay had one foot in each of Belinda's ears, Jason lay sprawled across Clay's belly, face up, arms over his head as if he'd fallen asleep while under arrest. Grant had his face buried next to Belinda's hip, looking like he was trying to suffocate himself. His knees were in his chest, his rump in the air.

Ace felt his heart perform that amazing miracle of clenching and swelling at the same time. It happened every time he realized how blessed he was, how much he loved those three little people that sprang, somehow, from his loins.

God, they were so perfect. And they were growing so fast. And he was so damn terrified that, housekeeper or not, he would never be smart enough, wise enough, patient enough...wouldn't be any of the things a man had to be to raise children on his own, without a woman beside him to soften the edges, teach them compassion, help guide them to manhood.

What am I supposed to do, Cathy? How am I supposed to do this without you?

There was no answer. There never was.

He went back to the kitchen and picked up the phone. "Sorry, Elaine, they fell asleep."

"Seeing Aunt Binda must have worn them out," she said with a fond smile in her voice.

"Yeah. Her, too. They're sprawled all over her, and all four of them are out."

Elaine laughed. "Well, you tell them I called to thank them for the balloons."

"They'll be sorry they missed you. I'll have them call you tomorrow evening."

"Good. And how are you doing, dear?"

"Me?" He shrugged. "I'm all right."

"Have you been dating anyone special?"

Ace didn't know whether to be shocked, amused, or angry. When the hell was he supposed to have time to see anyone, special or not? And why would he want to? "No," was all he said.

"Ace, dear, you need to get out, kick up your heels. You're way too young to stop living. Cathy wouldn't like to think of you spending the rest of your life alone, you know that."

That was quite a leap, Ace thought, from dating, to the rest of his life. "I haven't stopped living," he protested.

"I hope not. You should think about remarrying. It's been two years, Ace."

"Elaine…"

"I know, it's none of my business. Just think about it."

"Yes, ma'am." He asked about her husband, Howard, and after a few more minutes they hung up.

Hell. His wife's mother wanted him to find a new

wife. "Get real, Elaine," he muttered. He needed a new wife like he needed more sagebrush.

Yeah, smart guy, and you were just worrying about how to raise the boys without a woman beside you. There's the answer. Get remarried.

Bad idea, he knew. He wasn't ready for a move like that. Besides, he knew every woman in the county, and he couldn't see himself getting mixed up with any of them. Not that there was anything wrong with them. Wyatt County had some damn fine women—what few women it had. He just wasn't interested in dating, let alone getting remarried.

Shaking his head at Elaine's ridiculous suggestion, and at himself for even thinking about it, he headed back to the living room. There were three little boys he knew who belonged in bed.

One by one, Ace carried his sleeping sons upstairs to their room. With all three tucked in for the night, he uttered a quick, silent prayer of thanks and another for guidance. He wanted his sons raised with love and laughter, rather than beneath the iron rule of their father, the way he had been.

He was not, Ace assured himself, like King Wilder. Would not be. Could not be.

And on that pleasant note he turned and went back downstairs.

What was he supposed to do about Belinda? Leave her asleep in the chair? Wake her up? He was sure that if the situation were reversed and he was the one asleep in the chair, she would find some diabolical way to wake him. Ice water in his face, maybe. Or his lap.

She lay there, looking every bit the beautiful angel—which awake, she most certainly wasn't. It dawned on him, as he stood watching her sleep, that he had never seen her motionless before. Not once, in the ten years he'd known her.

He remembered the day they met. Hell, it was his and Cathy's wedding rehearsal. Who wouldn't remember that? The sister of the bride had narrowed her eyes and looked him up and down.

"I don't trust men like you," she'd said. "If you hurt my sister, I'll have to kill you."

Before Ace had had a chance to defend himself and assure her he had no intention of ever deliberately hurting the woman he loved, Cathy had stepped between them and smiled sweetly. "Be nice, Belinda." Cathy always smiled sweetly.

Never had Ace seen two sisters so different. In looks, in attitude, in temperament.

With a bittersweet ache in his chest, he glanced at the ten-by-twelve framed photo of Cathy on the wall. He didn't need it, of course, to remember her. She was in his heart still, and always would be. So beautiful, with her creamy skin and pale blond hair to the middle of her back, her quiet blue eyes and soft, smiling mouth. Dainty, petite. The top of her head had barely reached his collarbone. So soft, so sweet, so loving. Ace had never heard her raise her voice or utter a harsh word to anyone. She had been, quite simply, the warmest, most giving person he'd ever known. When she had died she'd left a hole in his heart and in his life that would never be filled.

Then, he thought with a twist of his lips, there was Belinda. Two years older than Cathy, she'd taken her coloring from their father rather than from their mother, as Cathy had. Her skin was darker, more gold than cream. She wore her black hair short, and her gray eyes were the color of angry thunderheads. At least when she was sniping at him, which was nearly all the time they were around each other.

Belinda was opinionated, hardheaded, as strong-willed as a U.S. Marine drill sergeant. She would argue with a fence post just for the fun of arguing.

He shook his head. So different from Cathy.

But Belinda could be soft. She was soft with his sons. There was no mistaking the love in those turbulent gray eyes when she looked at her nephews.

Too bad her marriage a few years back hadn't worked out. Maybe having children of her own would have mellowed her some. It certainly wasn't too late for her to have a family of her own, he thought. She was only thirty-three. A lot of women waited until their thirties these days before starting a family.

But it would take a hell of a man, he thought, to take her on. He'd have to be the most secure, self-assured man in the world, or she'd cut him to ribbons with that sharp tongue of hers.

That, Ace decided, was not fair of him. Belinda got along great with Jack and Trey. Sure, she and Trey razzed each other, but it was all in fun. Unlike some of her more biting comments toward him.

With a sigh, Ace squatted next to the recliner. They needed a truce. *He* needed it. He'd had enough strife in his life. He wanted a little peace in his home these days. Maybe if he tried being nicer to her…

"Belinda," he said softly. "Hey, Aunt Binda, wake up."

No reaction.

"Slim." He reached out and placed his hand on her arm, and realized, at once, that it was possibly the first time he'd ever touched her, and equally possible that it was the biggest mistake of his life.

She felt the touch, even through her sleep. It was warm and gentle. The hand was large and rough. And it shot a hot spark straight up her arm and down to her heels.

Belinda came awake slowly, savoring the spark of sharp sexual awareness. She blinked, and Ace's face came into focus. In that instant, with his hand on her arm and her blood humming hot and fast in her veins, truth burst through her. A terrible truth. All these years, all the tension she felt, the jittery sensation in the pit of her stomach, the vulnerability that made her so angry—all of it circled back and slammed the breath from her lungs. Sexual attraction.

Guilt. Shame. Fury. She nearly choked on them. *Belinda Randall is attracted to her sister's husband.*

And he knew. He had to know. Why else would he be looking at her with all the horror she felt inside at the mere idea that she could want him?

Without bothering to lower the footrest, she scrambled out of the recliner and raced upstairs to her room. For the second time that day, she braced her back against the closed door and slid to the floor. But this time there was no sense of relief that she'd managed to survive another round with him. This time there was only panic.

In retrospect it all made a terrible kind of sense. The off-center feeling she got around Ace, the jitters. Perhaps subconsciously she'd recognized those things for what they were, and that was why she seemed to always be on the attack around him. A built-in defense mechanism to keep a nice, sharp distance between her and her sister's husband.

If it wasn't so pathetic, she might have laughed. Hysterically. If it wasn't so ridiculous, she might have wept.

He'd seen. Oh, God, Ace had seen her reaction—she knew he had. What was she going to do? She couldn't admit it. Not ever. He would laugh in her face.

And why not? The idea that he might be attracted right back was laughable. After Cathy, with her pretty blond looks, her soft shapely body, her one desire in life to please her man—what would any man want with Belinda after having had a woman like Cathy? Belinda wasn't pretty, wasn't blond. Her body was thin, with sharp angles instead of curves. She didn't have any hips to speak of, and most of the measurement around her chest was ribs.

She wasn't quiet, wasn't graceful, and she had more important things to think about than whether or not she could see her reflection in her freshly waxed floor.

The bitter tone to her own thoughts brought Belinda up short. Okay, so she'd always been a little envious—all right, since nobody was listening, *pea-green* with envy—of her sister's looks, popularity, the way all the boys in school—and later, the men—flocked around Cathy, all but drooling over her.

From the time they had been small children, the pattern had been set. Belinda had been "Mama and Daddy's little sweetheart." Cathy was "Mama and Daddy's pretty little angel."

Everybody knew angels were nicer, prettier, more important than sweethearts. When friends and family came over, everyone always made a fuss over how pretty Cathy was. Belinda had been complimented on her intelligence. She'd been proud of that, taking it as a high compliment, until she realized it was meant as a sop. Then, in her young mind, it became a slap in the face, leaving her feeling inferior in every way.

As the girls had grown, nothing much changed. Things only got worse, the wounds deeper. Cathy played the title role in *Snow White* and *Sleeping Beauty*. Belinda was a witch-like troll under the bridge in *Three Billy Goats Gruff*.

Cathy was head cheerleader and homecoming queen; she had a date every Friday and Saturday night from junior high on, and her class studies centered around home ec. Belinda captained the debate team, was president of the student council, and excelled in math. Her first date was with geeky George Lembowsky, and only then because neither had a better offer for the senior prom.

Cathy married a man most women would kill to get their hands on. A tall, sexy cowboy with his own ranch and who brought with him no parents-in-law to interfere. Belinda had married a twerp who expected her to support him in comfort for the rest of his life.

Cathy produced three beautiful sons. Belinda produced a miscarriage, followed shortly by an ugly divorce.

Now, here she was, coveting everything that had been Cathy's—her three beautiful sons and their father—and it made her sick. A man who'd had Cathy Randall for his wife wouldn't want anything to do with Belinda.

And what the dickens was she thinking about that for, anyway? She pushed away from the door and started pacing. Good God, her sister's husband. How low could she get? It didn't matter that Cathy had been gone for two years. Ace would always belong to Cathy. How could a man ever forget such a sweet, loving angel? Such a perfect woman?

The realization of her own feelings for Ace had Belinda turning toward the closet to reach for her suitcases. Then she stopped. She couldn't leave the boys. They were all that was left of a sister who, despite the envy, Belinda had always loved.

Maybe Belinda had always envied Cathy her husband and children, too. Maybe that was why Belinda had rushed into her own disastrous marriage.

Okay, so maybe there was no *maybe* to it. Belinda had known exactly what she was doing when she married, of all people, Todd the Bod. Because he had dated Cathy. Belinda had been trying to prove to herself that she could have everything Cathy had. Be everything Cathy was. Be adored. Like Cathy.

What a joke. Only perfect people—like Cathy—had perfect lives. Belinda was about as far from perfect as she could get, and she knew it.

All right. She took a slow breath, then let it out. She would stay, and she would act as though nothing had happened. Because nothing had. Nor would it ever.

Now that she was finished feeling sorry for herself, the furious anger that she'd felt briefly downstairs came rushing back. Anger at herself, for allowing herself to feel an attraction, however fruitless and humiliating, for the man she held responsible for her sister's death.

Chapter Three

It was a fluke. That's what Ace told himself all night long. Static electricity. His overactive imagination. He hadn't really felt a spark of attraction when he'd touched Belinda last night.

He stopped outside the back door, set the milk pails down on the sidewalk and stuffed his hands into his jacket pockets. The eastern sky was turning gray. It was chilly now, with the sun not yet up, but it would be a warm day.

She was in there, in the kitchen. He could hear her rattling around, probably breaking out a box of Cocoa Puffs to feed him and the crew for breakfast. She was that ornery, this sister-in-law of his. If she'd asked Clay, there would be chocolate syrup to go with the cereal. He wondered, with a shake of his head, if he would ever get a real meal again in his own house without having to cook it himself.

He would just stand here a minute and get his head on straight. And stop thinking about her.

For crying out loud, she was Cathy's sister. The Wicked Witch of the West.

All he'd done was place his hand on her forearm. There had been no zing in his blood, no speeding of his pulse. His mouth had not gone dry. And even if they had, it was only a fluke.

That settled, he picked up the milk pails and entered the mudroom. There he set the pails on top of the freezer chest and turned to reach for the straining-cloth and gallon jars on the shelf by the door to the kitchen. That's when he saw her.

Hell. Another fluke.

No way, he told himself. No way in hell this woman was getting to him. Her short black hair had that sleep-mussed look, and as near as he could tell, she didn't have on a lick of makeup. She wore a blue-and-white Mickey Mouse T-shirt three sizes too large for her slender frame, and baggy gray sweatpants. Above her bare feet, the cuffs were frayed. No way did the sight of those bare feet and that tousled hair get to him.

From out in the yard he heard the men approaching. With a muttered curse, he draped the cheesecloth over the first wide-mouthed jar and snapped a rubber band around the mouth to hold the cloth in place while he poured the milk from the first pail.

He did not, most definitely did not, have the hots for his wife's sister. The knot in his gut was hunger. For food. Because he hadn't eaten. The slight tremor in his hands was from a lack of sleep and too much caffeine.

Or terror.

"Hot damn, something sure smells good." Trey stepped into the mudroom from outside and blew on his hands. With Jack and the other men crowding up behind him, he paused in the doorway and took a deep breath. "Ahh. Sausage."

"No way." Jack shoved him on through and stepped inside. "That's bacon I smell."

"If you two yahoos would get out of the way, I'd like a smell of that, too," complained Stoney.

Relief eased the tension that had tightened Ace's shoulders. Now he wouldn't have to face Belinda alone.

Coward.

No, just cautious, he told himself. From the look on her face last night when he woke her up, she'd known exactly what had been racing through his mind. She wouldn't stand for that. Not from him. She was liable to chew him up and spit him out.

Still, he thought, as he poured the second pail of milk into the second gallon jar, that didn't explain the way she had scrambled out of the chair as if she'd suddenly discovered it was on fire. Surely she hadn't been afraid he was going to jump her bones right there in the living room. Surely she hadn't been afraid of anything.

So why, he asked himself, his eyes narrowed in thought as he screwed the lids onto the jars of milk, for just an instant, before she'd glared at him in anger, had she looked terrified?

"Good morning, gentlemen," she said.

Ace hung his jacket on a peg and stepped into the kitchen.

"You, too, Ace," she added with a smirk.

A round of snickers made its way through the men as they took their seats.

Well, Ace thought, so much for worrying about things being different between them. It looked like it was business—and her smart mouth—as usual. The relief that loosened the knot in his gut almost made him smile. Until he thought to worry about what, exactly, she'd fixed for breakfast.

The huge stack of waffles, piles of bacon and sausage, and a giant bowl of scrambled eggs complete with bell peppers, onions, and mushrooms, came as a pleasant surprise.

Trey, already seated at the table, reached for the platter of waffles with a laugh. "And here I was worried all we'd get would be Frosted Flakes."

"Oh, ye of little faith," Belinda cried. "Would I do that to hungry working men? Never mind." She held up one hand, palm out. "Don't answer that."

It took all of Belinda's willpower to keep from snarling. If she'd gotten more than ten minutes' sleep last night, she'd kiss a goat on the lips. And there was Ace, his cheeks ruddy from the cold and those Wilder blue eyes staring at her as if they could see right through her skull and read every thought she'd ever had.

She turned away and started filling the men's coffee cups. It did nothing for her peace of mind to realize that she knew the instant Ace took his gaze off her and looked away.

What a stupid thing to feel—a man's gaze. And the loss of it.

While he washed up at the sink, she took her seat at the table and started filling her plate.

"You sure make a fine breakfast, Miss Belinda," Stoney said.

"Why, thank you, sir." She gave him a big grin. "I guess last night's supper had you a little worried."

The flush that stained the old man's cheeks was cute. "No such thing," he protested. "There weren't a thing in the world wrong with last night's supper, and that's a fact."

"I'm glad you liked it."

"Yes, ma'am, it was just fine."

"Shut up, Stoney," Ace muttered as he took his seat. "Before we end up with—"

"Shut up yourself," Jack complained. "Don't give anybody any ideas, huh?"

Ace ran his tongue around his teeth. "I get your point, bro. This looks really good, Belinda. Oh, there's two gallons of milk sitting out on the freezer." He took his usual seat at the head of the table. "They probably ought to go in the fridge as soon as possible."

Belinda narrowed her eyes. "You carried the damn milk all the way from the barn and couldn't make it from the mudroom to the kitchen?"

"I carried it all the way from the barn and strained it. You can't carry it the last twenty feet?"

"Now, children." Trey tapped his fork against his plate. "Play nice."

With twin snarls, Belinda and Ace turned on him, ready to pounce.

"God," Trey said to Belinda as he reached for the bowl of eggs. "You're gorgeous when you're angry."

Belinda sputtered, then burst out laughing at the sheer stupidity of his clichéd comment. "Lord, Number Three, they don't let you off this ranch often enough. Just shut up and eat your breakfast.''

Trey's grin would have been angelic were it not for the devil in his eyes. ''Yes, ma'am. Pass the sausage, will ya, Stoney?''

The men plowed through breakfast as if they were famine victims at a feast. With the boys not there to need attention, conversation was nonexistent. Instead of asking for the saltshaker, they pointed. Thanks were issued in low grunts. If Belinda hadn't been quick on the uptake, they would have polished off all the food before she'd gotten her share.

But afterward Ace was all too talkative for her peace of mind when he gave out the day's instructions. Jack was to ride up to check the grass on the land they leased from the government up in the mountains. The rest of the men, including Trey because they were shorthanded, would either be checking fence, or mending what fence they already knew needed mending. All of that translated into the fact that none of them would make it back to the house for lunch. Belinda had less than twenty minutes to come up with enough sandwiches for them to take to tide them over until supper.

''Great,'' she muttered to herself after the men left the house. She ignored the dirty breakfast dishes still on the table and started slicing the ham she had planned to heat for the noon meal. Here she'd been planning on being the perfect little housekeeper—*why* escaped her just then—by having them a hot lunch ready. So much for glazed ham and sweet potatoes, she thought glumly.

There was no time to brew tea, so she made instant for iced tea for their remaining thermoses. They'd already filled several with coffee and taken them with them.

They needed something other than just sandwiches.

No help for it. The boys would have to do without potato chips for a while. She grabbed the bags of chips she'd bought the day before and added them to the men's lunches. For good measure, she added an apple and a package of cupcakes to each lunch.

"Next time," she muttered to herself as she wrapped sandwiches in plastic wrap and slapped them into lunch boxes, "a little warning might be nice."

"I'm sorry."

At the unexpected sound of Ace's voice from right behind her, Belinda shrieked and dropped an apple on the floor. "You scared the life out of me." Her heart was nearly jumping out of her chest. She placed a hand there to hold it in place. "I thought you were outside."

"I was." He shrugged. His gaze dipped to the hand over her chest. His brain chose that moment to remind him that she never wore a bra. As if he needed a reminder. He jerked his gaze away. "Then I realized that I shouldn't have just sprung lunch on you that way. I came back in to apologize."

"Okay." Her heart started to slow back down to a normal pace. "Okay." What the devil did he think he was doing, looking at her chest that way? "Fine. I've about got everything ready."

"And I wanted to thank you for breakfast."

"Had you worried about Frosted Flakes, did I?"

His lips twitching, he folded his arms across his chest. "I was betting on Cocoa Puffs."

She would not be charmed by him, Belinda vowed.

"Anyway, thanks. It was terrific."

"You in the habit of thanking your housekeeper for breakfast?"

"You're not my housekeeper. And it was about the best breakfast I ever remember having."

"My, my. A compliment?"

His eyes narrowed. "And a thank-you. You've had them before."

Belinda turned back toward the counter and reached for another apple. "Not from you."

"You've never cooked my breakfast before."

"You like that, huh?" She peered at him over her shoulder. "The little woman playing Susie Home-maker for you?"

"No need to get testy. I was hungry—the food was good. That's all." He turned and headed for the door. "Just put the lunches out on the freezer. We'll stop by and pick them up on our way out."

Her fingers squeezed around the apple in her hand. "Ace?"

In the doorway he stopped and looked back.

Stupid, she told herself. Stupid to call his name just to have him turn and look back at her. Just to see his face again. What was she supposed to say now? The alert, half-expectant look in his eyes had her nerves humming.

Ace looked at her, with her baggy clothes, her bare feet, her tousled hair, and wanted to curse. Nothing about her, absolutely nothing, should be causing this stirring in his loins. When she called his name, he had no business turning back expectantly, eagerly, just for another look at her before heading out for the day.

"Yeah?" he finally said, fighting the ridiculous

urge to cross that kitchen floor again and smooth that hair down just to see if she'd let him.

The way she licked her lips had him curling his hands into fists.

"Uh, how late do the boys usually sleep?"

He breathed in slowly, then let it out. "Till around eight or nine, thereabouts." Before he could do something really stupid, he stomped out the back door.

Belinda refused to stare at the empty doorway like some love-starved idiot. She had more important things to do than moon over some man—any man, much less Ace Wilder.

Feeling something moist and sticky on her fingers, she looked down to find a mangled apple in her hand, her fingernails buried deep into its flesh.

Oh, Lord. She had to get away from here just as soon as she could. Tonight she would hit him up about the ad for a housekeeper. Surely even in this sparsely populated area of the globe there was a capable woman who needed a steady job.

She finished slamming together the lunches and carried them to the freezer in the mudroom, then hauled the two gallon jars of milk to the refrigerator. She was halfway through clearing the breakfast table when the men, one by one, came for their lunches.

All except Ace. Jack picked up Ace's lunch for him. "Don't let those little rascals upstairs run you ragged," he called to her.

"Not a chance," she called back.

At the barn Ace snatched his lunch from Jack and tossed it onto the seat of the truck.

"You're welcome," Jack muttered.

All he got in response was a growl.

"You wanna tell me what's eating you all of a sudden?"

"Nothing's eating me."

"Nothing should be." But Jack would prod until he found out what it was. "Belinda's here to look after the boys and the house. That takes a load off you, doesn't it?"

"Yeah." It should, Ace thought. "It takes a load off. Let's get a move on. We're burning daylight, bro."

"Right." Jack turned away and headed for his rig. He wasn't through with the subject, but Ace was right. Even with knocking a couple of hours off his trip by trailering his horse as far as he could before mounting up, he'd be all day getting up to the high grazing land and back. "See you tonight."

"Yeah." Tonight, Ace thought. When he'd have to go back into his house and she'd be there. Dammit, that wasn't supposed to be a problem. Wouldn't be, he promised himself. Wasn't. It was just a fluke.

Okay, two flukes now. But no more.

The boys, once they were up, did not run Belinda ragged. It was all the other chores that went with the job that nearly did it. That and the battle over breakfast.

Belinda had never asserted any authority over her nephews. Always before, she was one of them, taking their side against the other adults always telling them what to do.

"But I want my Cocoa Puffs," Jason complained, his lower lip sticking out.

"Frosted Flakes." Clay folded his arms across his

chest in such a perfect imitation of Ace that Belinda didn't know whether to laugh or scream.

Grant put in his two cents' worth. "Fwosty Puffs."

"The men ate eggs," she tried.

"They prob'ly ate 'em all," Jason offered with a gleam in his eye. "There's prob'ly nuthin' left but Cocoa Puffs."

"Nice try, kid." She ruffled his hair. "Eat your eggs, and if you want cereal after that, we'll renegotiate."

"What's that?" Jason asked suspiciously.

"It means we'll talk about it. After you eat your eggs."

"Daddy lets us eat cereal," Clay stated.

"Daddy lets us," Grant mimicked.

She gave all three of them a narrow-eyed look. "How about your Aunt Mary? What did she fix you for breakfast?"

They ate their eggs.

Afterward she settled them before that perennial parental favorite of baby-sitters, the television, while she made the beds, then went down to the basement and started on the laundry.

There wasn't much of it, she noticed. The pile beneath the laundry chute didn't contain much more than the clothes they'd tossed down last night. Ace must have handled that little chore recently.

Still, there was no use letting it pile up. Three sets of little-boy clothes, plus what Ace had worn yesterday, plus a pair of his red sweatpants. She dumped them all into the washer, added laundry soap and made a mental note to come back down in a half hour to transfer everything to the dryer.

Back upstairs there was supper to plan, a kitchen

floor to mop. She was ready to swear that more food had ended up on the floor than in the boys' mouths.

When the floor was clean and she caught herself staring at it with pride and a sense of accomplishment, she nearly choked.

"This won't do," she muttered to herself. "This won't do at all."

Deciding it was time for a reality check, she grabbed her laptop and followed the boys outside. While they played cowboy in the front yard, with Scooter serving as their faithful and ever-patient horse, Belinda settled onto the wooden swing on the covered veranda with her computer. She made notes and roughed out a couple of web-site designs for the bid she was working on for a potential new client.

She was good at her job, and loved the independence that working on the Internet allowed her. Give her a modem and she could work anywhere. Even, she thought, looking out at the endless expanse of rolling land dotted with sagebrush, the wilds of Wyoming.

She remembered with humor her own naiveté about the size of the ranch when she'd first learned that Cathy was marrying a rancher and moving to Wyoming. "Big" was how Cathy had described it.

Knowing nothing about ranches and caring even less, Belinda had figured maybe a square mile. Or, just to be generous—not to mention ridiculous—maybe, if the ranch were in the shape of a square, it might be two miles by two miles. Four square miles. Which sounded outrageous. No ranch would be that big.

Then she'd paid her first visit, about six months after Cathy and Ace were married. Shock was the only word to describe what she'd felt upon learning that the Flying Ace Ranch actually encompassed roughly thirty thousand deeded acres, more than forty-six square miles. And that wasn't counting the grazing land up in the mountains, leased from the U.S. Forest Service.

Forty-six square miles. Unbelievable that any one man—or family, in this case—could own that much land.

Who else would want it? Then she'd seen it—sagebrush as far as the eye could see—and she thought, Why shouldn't one family own it all?

But it grew on you, so to speak, that sagebrush. Seeped into a person's senses with its pungent smell, its soft gray-green color, its strength and persistence even in the face of drought, and stayed there. Thriving, it seemed.

There was more than sagebrush here, though, she'd learned during her subsequent visits. There was grass out there on that deceptively flat-looking range, sparse, but good feed for cattle. There were ravines and gullies, dry most of the time, but sometimes funneling a wall of water down on the unwary during heavy rain. There were ice-cold streams of snowmelt tumbling down out of the Wyoming Mountains to the west, joining up with those that ran from the Wind River Range to the northeast, all of them, sooner or later, emptying into the Green River.

There were thick stands of cottonwoods and willows along the streams where, in the early spring, moose went to calve. Small herds of antelope mixed themselves in with the cattle now and then, and elk tore down the fences every chance they got.

At first Belinda had been baffled by Cathy's casual

acceptance of the isolation. After all, it was two miles of dirt road just to get from the house to the ranch gate, then another thirteen to the nearest pavement. From there it was thirty-two miles of two-lane blacktop to town.

Town. Big whoopee. The town of Hope Springs— the only town in Wyatt County—boasted a scant twenty-two hundred citizens. The entire county wasn't much more than that, either. Imagine, an entire county with only thirty-five hundred people, while the cattle, she was told, usually numbered around forty thousand.

There'd been more than thirty-five hundred people in her high school, Belinda thought.

But each time she had come to visit over the years, she had grown to appreciate this least-populated area of the country. After the smog and clog of Denver, it was a nice change. The air here was so clean it practically crackled, and it was quiet, if you didn't count the cattle, the coyotes, the crickets and frogs.

Then there was the sky, so vivid and blue that it hurt the eyes. That wide Wyoming sky that went on forever and ever, until, in the west, it gave way to rocky, jagged mountaintops.

She sat looking out at that sky, at the jagged, snow-covered peaks, the rugged rangeland, at the three young boys tumbling over each other, giggling, chasing the dog then running from him, and set her work aside. This was too good a day to miss.

Behind her, around her, she felt the house, tall and sturdy, with fresh white paint and deep-green shutters. Built by King Wilder, left to his children, who would undoubtedly leave it to their children.

The rest of the ranch—the land, barns, sheds, stables, indoor arena, the maze of corrals, crops, equipment, even the occasional oil or gas well dotting the range in the distance—all of it stood silent testament to a family's persistence through the generations.

But in addition to the Flying Ace and all it entailed, King Wilder had passed to his children his black hair and blue eyes and a love of the land—of this land—and of ranching. They were all here, Ace, Jack, Trey. Rachel might be away at college, but she would be coming back and opening her veterinary practice in Hope Springs. She would probably live here on the ranch. It was her home.

Belinda considered the house where she had grown up to be her home. Her parents had made it that way. But the house had been built for them; there was no history there. That was the difference.

History. Tradition. There was a lot of tradition in ranching. It was something Belinda rarely thought about, being usually caught up in the new, the latest technology. But here on the Flying Ace she could feel the tradition. She pictured in her mind the family cemetery up on the hill to the west, where Cathy was buried alongside her children's Wilder ancestors. And somewhere Ace was out there, probably on horseback, herding cattle the way his great-grandfather had. Then there were his sons, who would most likely do the same one day soon. The carrying on, the handing down. If it had seemed stifling to her, now there was also an odd comfort to it that she'd never thought of before.

The day sped by faster than she would have expected. She'd set her work aside and rolled on the grass with the boys, followed them to the chicken house and helped them gather eggs, and fed them lunch. While they were down for a nap, she remembered the laundry and went to the basement and threw the load into the dryer, then back up to her room to put in some serious time on the computer while the boys slept.

All in all, a full day, she thought, as she put two chuck roasts into the oven for supper.

If she watched the clock a little too often and wondered when the men would be back, it was only because she wanted to time the meal to be ready on time. That was all.

Terrific. Now he had her lying to herself.

She had to get out of here. As much as she loved her nephews, she had to get off this ranch and away from Ace Wilder.

"So what's the word, Jack?"

Jack took his time savoring his first bite of roast beef. Although Ace directed the question at him, older brother's eyes were locked on to Belinda like a hawk on prey.

So that's the way the wind was blowing, Jack thought with a small smile. Yes, sir, it was going to get real interesting around this place, it surely was.

When Jack merely stared at his plate and didn't answer, Ace realized he himself was staring at Belinda, watching her avoid meeting his gaze. Realizing it, he looked over at Jack. "Well?"

"The word," Jack said, "is *fair.* Still some snow in the pass. We could move the herd up there now if we had to. Snow's melted back to the tree line in the valley, and the grass up there looks good. But it'd be better if we waited another week or ten days."

"All right." Ace looked down at his plate. The

roast was so tender it fell apart at a touch of his fork. "We'll start gathering the herd the end of next week. You get that fence fixed?" he asked Trey.

"Nah," Trey said lazily, leaning back in his chair. "I thought it looked good down. We've got too many cattle, anyway."

Jason, the only one of the boys listening, giggled.

"All right," Ace conceded. "Stupid question." He turned to his sons. "What did you boys do today? Grant, you're supposed to eat the carrots, not throw them at Clay."

Belinda watched as Ace listened to his sons regaling him with their day. He was a good father, she admitted, the way he showed genuine interest in each of them, paid attention to what they said, asked them questions and got them to eat cooked carrots.

She wasn't surprised, of course. She'd seen him with his sons from the day each of them had been born. She'd known him for ten years, had seen him as a good father, a loving husband, a smart, dedicated rancher.

So why did she suddenly feel as if she didn't know him at all? Why did the sight of him fresh from the shower as he'd come to the table have her wanting to take a towel to his hair to finish drying it for him? Why couldn't she meet his gaze when he looked at her?

Why the hell was he looking at her, anyway?

This wouldn't do. It wouldn't do at all.

After supper the other men left for the night, and Ace spent time with the boys while she cleaned up the kitchen. It wasn't until after bath time and their last half hour of television that Ace put them to bed, grabbed himself a beer from the refrigerator and made his way to his office.

That's when she braced herself and cornered him. "I'd like to talk to you."

Ace looked up from the pile of mail on his desk to find her standing in the doorway of his office. Dammit, he'd come in here to get away from her.

To hide, you coward.

All right, to hide.

"What about?" he asked, cursing the hoarseness in his voice. Hoarseness brought on by the sudden kick to his libido.

"I'd like to know what you're doing about finding a housekeeper."

"Tired of the job already?"

Ignoring his question, she crossed to the chair before his desk and sat down. "Do you have an ad in the paper?"

"In the county paper, yeah. I've had one in for two weeks."

"Any response?"

"Nothing that worked out."

"You have a copy of this ad?"

"Sure." He picked up the *Wyatt County Gazette* from the corner of his desk and handed it to her. It was folded open to the classifieds.

Belinda read the ad and shook her head. "Obviously this isn't working."

"You can do better?"

She shrugged. "Maybe." Definitely, since advertising was her specialty. "Tell me what kind of person you're looking for. I'll see what I can do with it."

Ace leaned back in his chair. "I want a woman—"

"Do you, now?"

"Do you want to hear this or not?"

"I asked, didn't I?"

He ground his teeth together. "I want a woman—"

"Why a woman? Why not a man? Maybe an older man, grandfather type."

Ace shook his head. "We've got plenty of men around here already, and Stoney's almost as much of a grandfather to the boys as your dad is. They need the care of a woman. Someone to balance things out for them, teach them the softer side of life, if you will."

"A man can't do that?"

"You want me to hire a man?"

"I'm just asking. I'm curious, that's all."

"My boys need to hear a softer voice, feel a softer touch, a smooth hand now and then," he said, looking down at his hands. "Instead of one rough with calluses. They won't have any trouble learning the harder side of life out here. But they need to know about the softer side, too. I want a woman to teach them that."

"Sounds to me like you're after a mother for them, not a housekeeper."

"They have a mother," he said tightly.

Belinda glanced down at her lap and picked at the ragged edge of her thumbnail. "Had, Ace. Had."

He ran a hand over his face. "Right. But if I ever decide to find them a new one, I won't be doing it through an ad in the paper. What I need right now is a housekeeper."

"I have an idea I'd like you to consider."

Leery, he dropped his hand to the desk. "What?"

"While you look for this housekeeper, why don't

I take the boys back to Colorado with me? That would free up some of your time and—''

"No."

"—you wouldn't have to worry about them."

"Not only *no,* but *hell, no.* My boys stay here, with me."

"It was just a thought." And a desperate one, she acknowledged.

"Only one full day and you're ready to hightail it back to the big city, huh?''

"It's not that."

"Then why did you bring it up? You knew what I'd say."

"I just thought it might make things easier on you."

"Bull."

"I beg your pardon?"

"Make things easier on me, my foot. There's not an altruistic, or even cooperative, bone in your body and we both know it. You just want out of here."

Her eyes narrowed to steel-gray slits. "I'll stick, cowboy, but you better find somebody, and fast. You're fresh out of Aunt Marys who'll come in and save your butt this time around."

"What the hell do you expect me to do? Hang the boys from a hook on the wall because I can't find anybody to hire?"

Belinda closed her eyes and took in a deep breath for patience. Then she took a second. And a third. "Look. I love those boys, every single one of them. I wouldn't for my life wish any of them hadn't been born. But dammit, Ace, what were you trying to do, populate the world? Prove what a stud you are? Why did you need three children? Weren't two enough?

Especially after the warnings with the second? The third time around killed my sister. Since the only person around here responsible for that is you, you better start figuring a way out of this latest mess you've gotten yourself into.''

If she had picked up his letter opener and stabbed him in the heart, it might have hurt less. ''You don't know what you're talking about.''

''Don't I? My sister is dead, and those three little boys are without a mother. I hold you personally responsible. Now do something about it, damn you.''

''You listen to me—''

''No.'' Belinda held up a hand to cut him off. ''I've already said more than I should. If you say what you're thinking, I'm liable to say something back that will make it impossible for the two of us to share the same house. I'll be damned if I'll let you cart those boys off to some day care somewhere just so you and I don't have to look at each other.''

''If I was willing to cart them off to some day care somewhere, we *wouldn't* be looking at each other. But don't you ever—'' he jabbed a finger in her face ''—bring up my marriage to your sister again. What passed between us was private and none of your damn business. I don't care how much she may have told you about us, you don't know what the hell you're talking about, so just shut up.''

''You want me to shut up? I'll shut up. But you get somebody out here, and you get them out here fast. And in the meantime,'' she added hotly, ''keep your damn hands to yourself. Don't touch me again like you did last night when I was asleep.''

When Ace heard her feet pounding up the stairs, he looked down at his hands and saw them shaking.

Damn her. Damn them both.

Damn all three of them. Belinda, him, and Cathy.

He set his beer aside and went in search of something stronger.

Chapter Four

Neither Ace nor Belinda slept that night.

Ace was too full of fury. Of self-blame and painful memories.

Those same feelings kept Belinda awake, also. Some of her fury was self-directed; she shouldn't have said anything to Ace about Cathy and babies. There was no point in it. Yes, she blamed him, felt him responsible for Cathy's death, but whatever he'd done, she knew he hadn't done it to kill his wife.

God, why was life so damn complicated and confusing? And painful?

The men's work kept them around the headquarters the next day. After the boys were up and had eaten, Ace took them with him to the equipment shed so they could "help" him work on one of the rigs. He needed them with him, after last night's dredging up of the past. Needed to feel close to them. Needed to hold Grant, especially, to make sure his youngest son knew how much he was loved and wanted.

The rest of the men loved having the boys around. They were constantly stopping work to wander over and offer advice to Ace, slip candy to the boys. Tell tall tales.

After lunch Ace told the boys they would have to stay at the house with Belinda for the rest of the day. To give Belinda credit, she did not take it personally when they complained. Instead, she apparently recognized that they were still wound up from their morning with the men and suggested they go outside and play catch.

"I'll come out there with you as soon as I get the kitchen cleaned up," she promised.

As Ace started to follow the boys and the other men out the door, Belinda's voice stopped him.

"Ace, about last night."

"Don't."

"You were right," she said. "Whatever happened between you and Cathy is none of my business. But she was my sister, Ace, and I loved her."

"I know that." He paused, swallowed. "I loved her, too, Belinda." They stared at each other for a long moment, each feeling the loss of the woman who was no longer there. Each wondering where to go from here. "I loved her, too," he said again.

With Belinda's apology of sorts, Ace held hopes that the rest of the day would go as well as those two incidents.

It didn't.

He rode out to check on the herd in the south range

and found a calf stuck in a bog along the creek. By the time he'd roped the calf and pulled him out, he and the animal both were covered in thick mud up to their necks.

By the time he made it back to the barn, the mud had dried all over him. Trey, who'd been washing his rig, decided to help him out by hosing him down.

Then a stallion in the stallion barn decided to kick his stall door into splinters, and that had to be replaced right then. Afterward, the neighbor to the north called to report that a herd of elk had just taken down another section of Flying Ace fence. Terrific, Ace thought.

At least supper went off without a hitch. Afterward, Ace made it through bath time and TV with the boys. Thank God for the boys. They kept him grounded, even when the little devils were driving him insane. How were parents supposed to answer all those questions, meet all those youthful expectations?

After they finally turned in for the night, he closed himself in his office. To go over ranch records, he told himself.

To avoid a certain woman, his mind countered.

Okay, so he was avoiding her.

He stayed—hid—in the office until long after he heard her go upstairs. He spent most of that time searching for a missing invoice he knew he needed to pay, and not finding it. Frustrated, angry with himself, he finally gave up and called it a night.

Then he slept poorly, what little sleep he got. Who would have thought he would ever dream about Belinda Randall and satin sheets? Together. After waking up in a pool of sweat, guilt had kept him awake the rest of the night. Cathy's sister. Good grief, he'd had an erotic dream about his wife's sister.

He was, he decided, a disgusting creep, and the whole damn world sucked.

By the time he got up the next morning, his outlook had not improved. Then he opened his underwear drawer. Staring down at the contents, he didn't know whether to bellow with rage, whimper in defeat, or laugh like a loon.

Belinda came sharply awake at what sounded like the howl of a wild animal coming from down the hall. Her clock told her it was 4:30 a.m. It would have been pitch-black except for the greenish glow through her window from the utility light not too far from the house.

Her first concern was for the boys. Something had happened to the boys. Without a thought she jumped from the bed and threw open her door.

But the sound, she instantly realized, was not coming from the boys' room. It came from the end of the hall. Ace's room.

Heavens, it sounded like he had lost his mind in there. Was he... God, were those sobs? In five running leaps she was down the hall and flinging open his door. "Ace! Wha—"

Not sobs. Her heart slid back down from where it had lodged in her throat and settled in her chest, where it belonged. If it still beat too fast, it was because of irritation, plain and simple. She pushed the door shut behind her and marched toward the bed, where he lay sprawled on his back, hysterical with laughter.

"What's the matter with you? Quiet down before

you wake the boys." She had a bad moment an instant later when she realized that all he wore was a towel around his waist. She told herself not to be an idiot. The towel covered the essentials, didn't it?

Just because it left that wide, glorious chest bare, with its contour of muscles and its dusting of black hair, was no reason for her heart to jump. Nor were his bare arms, ropey with strength, nor those long, strong legs.

"Dammit, Ace." She jerked her gaze back up to his face. "Would you stop that and tell me what's so funny?"

He sat up and let out another gust of laughter, then stood. "I am. You are."

She narrowed her eyes at him. "What's that supposed to mean?"

"This." Laughing again, he dipped a hand into the open drawer of his dresser and came up with a pair of jockey shorts dangling from one finger. Pink jockey shorts.

Belinda bristled. "Well, how was I supposed to know those red sweatpants of yours would bleed all over your underwear?"

He hooted again, then grabbed her by the shoulders. "If nothing else, you'll keep me grounded in reality." Then he kissed her. Full on the mouth.

Belinda was so shocked, she couldn't think how to react. Couldn't think— That was it. She couldn't think at all. "What the hell did you do that for?"

Ace was asking himself the same question. He shouldn't have done it. Shouldn't have touched her at all, let alone kissed her. But before his brain could get the message to the rest of his body, or at least to his mouth to wipe out that intriguing taste of her, he

pulled her close and kissed her again. A real kiss this
time, openmouthed, with his tongue dipping in for a
better taste.

And heaven help him, she was suddenly kissing
him back.

If he was wearing nothing more than a towel, and
all she had on was a thin T-shirt that barely covered
the essentials, and if things just happened to get out
of hand, so be it. He wasn't in the mood to care. And
he wasn't laughing anymore. He was, suddenly, starving. For more of her. For all of her. He didn't know
where this had come from, or why. But just then he
couldn't see his way clear to caring. All he wanted
was more. Of her. Of Belinda.

It was the watery feeling in her knees that brought
Belinda to her senses. Never before had a man made
her knees go weak. More than slightly panicky, she
shoved at his chest and stepped back. She wiped the
back of her hand across her mouth and glared at him,
daring him to comment on the way her hand shook.
"What the hell was that for?" she demanded, not
caring if she was repeating herself.

Ace dropped his hands from her shoulders as if she
had suddenly burst into flames and scorched him.
"Damned if I know." And he'd be damned if he
knew why he wanted to do it again. The wanting
swamped him in guilt. Made him furious. "Get out
of here."

"Oh, that's rich." Cheeks flaming with shame,
with anger, she advanced on him. "I come in here
because you're making enough noise to wake the
dead, expecting to find you being attacked by a madman or something."

The closer she advanced, the faster Ace backed up.

"What were you going to do? Battle the madman with your bare hands?"

"You grab me and put the make on me, then tell *me* to get out? You're damn right I'll get out, cowboy."

"Rancher."

"I'll get the hell clear out of Dodge."

"Wait a minute." He snared her by the arm before she could jerk the door open.

"Let go of me."

"What do you mean you're getting the hell clear out of Dodge?"

"What do you think I mean, buckaroo? I said let go of me."

"You're running out? Running out on the boys?"

"Oh, yeah, lay a guilt trip on me."

Suddenly he did let go of her, as all the adrenaline disappeared and left him bewildered. "You're that scared of me that you'd hurt the boys that way?"

She snorted. "Don't flatter yourself." But he was right. She was that scared of him. Of herself. Of what she'd felt just now when he'd kissed her, when she'd kissed him back.

He turned away from her, hands low on his hips, his head hanging. Even to her jaded ears, his sigh sounded filled with self-disgust. "I'm sorry," he said. "I…"

"Oh, shut up. Put on your pink shorts before you lose that stupid towel. I've got breakfast to cook."

He whipped his head around. "You're staying?"

"Not for you, big boy. I'm staying for your sons, and because if I go home, my mother will get up out of her sickbed and drag herself up here. You just keep away from me, Ace Wilder. Just keep the hell away from me and go milk your damn cows."

* * *

Ace milked his damn cows. It wasn't a job the operator of a large ranch normally took upon himself. Usually it was given to the greenest hand—or a woman, but God help him if Belinda ever heard him make such a sexist remark—because milking cows wasn't considered macho enough for a real cowboy. But Ace liked it. Leaning his face against the warm side of the cow, hearing the milk fill the pail, sending a squirt now and then to the barn cats who stood by waiting. The quiet of it. The sameness of it. Those things worked together to soothe him, to start his day off with a good feeling.

Usually.

Today he didn't figure much of anything was going to soothe him, or ease the knot in his gut.

He'd kissed Belinda. Belinda Randall, of all people.

She was the first and only other woman he'd kissed since the day he met Cathy, more than ten years ago. He felt, he admitted, as if he'd just cheated on his wife.

And that was just plain ridiculous, he told himself. Cathy wouldn't expect him to spend the rest of his life alone. He hadn't really thought about it himself one way or the other. Hadn't been able to think about having a woman in his life again. But if anybody had asked him, he'd have had to admit that he sure never thought to spend the rest of his life celibate.

Hell, if a kiss made him feel this guilty, he'd never work his way up to making love.

Maybe it was just this particular woman he had a problem with. Belinda. Maybe if he went out and found himself another woman to kiss, someone who wasn't *his wife's sister,* for crying out loud, he wouldn't feel quite so much like a low-down, cheating son of a bitch.

It was a sad day when a man had to hang around the barn after the milking, waiting for the rest of the men to head for the house so he wouldn't have to face a woman when no one else was around.

Belinda and Ace tiptoed around each other, refusing to so much as make eye contact, much less speak to each other, during breakfast. It was the same again at lunch, when Ace, Trey and Jack were the only men there, the others having begged sandwiches from Belinda earlier to take out to the pastures with them.

They might have gone on that way for days, but for the shoving match Jason and Clay got into. Ace had taken the boys with him after lunch, hoping to give Belinda a little breathing room so the idea of leaving wouldn't crowd in on her again. He needed her, dammit. For the boys.

He was working with a two-year-old colt in the near corral. The boys were sitting on the ground just outside the corral fence watching. Ace didn't hear or see what started the shoving match, but he saw how it ended, when Jason shoved and Clay lost his balance and hit his head hard enough on the corral fence to make the steel post ring.

Ace's heart stopped. Just flat stopped when he heard the scream and saw the trickle of blood streaming down his middle son's face. Leaping from the colt's back, he vaulted over the fence and dropped to his knees in the dirt. "Let me see, Clay."

Clay was wailing loud enough to have the colt shying away to the other side of the corral. He kept both hands clamped over what Ace feared was already a growing knot on his forehead. The poor baby's face was beet-red and scrunched up in distress, with great racking sobs shaking his whole little body.

Ace wanted to cry with him. It ripped him apart when one of his babies got hurt.

Then Jason started crying. "I'm sorry, Clay, I'm s-sorry."

Then Grant, who probably didn't know why his brothers were crying but was scared because they were, started crying, too.

"Come on, Clay-boy, let me see your head."

"H-huuurt."

"I know, son, I know." Gently Ace tried to pry Clay's hands away. Ace was certainly no stranger to bumps on the head. Usually the injury was more painful than serious. But sometimes...

Footsteps pounded in from two directions as Jack and Trey came running.

"What happened?" Jack demanded.

"How bad is it?" Trey wanted to know.

"Fell and bumped his head," Ace said above the crying of all three boys. To Clay he said, "Let me see, now. I won't hurt it. Just let me take a look, okay?"

"No-o-o, Daddy, huuurrrt."

"Maybe I can help it stop hurting, but you have to let me look at it."

Finally Clay let Ace pry his hands away. Just below the hairline, above the outside corner of Clay's left eye, was a small, bloody scrape in the center of a large knot. "Good-looking goose egg," Ace said over the wailing. "Might even get a black eye."

Ace needed to get Clay to the house and clean him

up, get a better look at that bump before taking him in to the doctor to make sure everything was okay. He dreaded going up to the house. Aunt Mary had been steady as a rock, but Cathy had been a different story. Cathy, Lord love her, had been a panicker when it came to the everyday bumps and scrapes of little boys. Big boys, too, he thought, remembering the time he'd sliced the palm of his hand open. She'd fainted dead away at the sight of him bleeding over her kitchen sink. Jason had stepped on a nail once, and she hadn't fainted but she'd gotten hysterical.

Belinda being her sister, Ace feared he'd get the same reaction. She wasn't used to being around kids. Wouldn't realize that despite the tears and sobs, this really wasn't serious.

No help for it, though. "Come on, champ, let's get you up to the house and clean you up."

He doubted Clay heard him. The poor baby was too busy crying to hear much of anything. As were Jason and Grant.

Belinda heard the noise through her bedroom window. When Ace had taken the boys with him after lunch, she had gone to her computer and put in a couple of hours on the new web site she was designing. She was using a two-column layout with a side-bar for the main index page, and the product photos she had scanned were going to look spectacular with text flowing around them. She was trying to decide whether to add borders to the text when she heard the crying through her open window.

She jumped up and threw the curtains aside to look out. Her window faced the back of the house, and she had a clear view of the barns, garage and other buildings. The sight that greeted her wasn't one to smile over, but she couldn't help a slight quirk of her lips.

Side by side, three strapping, macho men strode up the dirt and gravel drive, each carrying a crying little boy.

God, she thought. *Look at them. They're magnificent.*

But as she raced from her room and down the stairs, she thought, Those poor babies. And she wasn't sure if she meant the three little boys who were crying, or the three men, who looked like they wanted to.

Ace entered the kitchen first, and she saw at once the blood on Clay's face.

"What happened?" she demanded as she pulled a clean rag from the drawer and wet it under the faucet.

Ace pulled out a chair from the table and sat, with Clay on his lap. While he told her what had happened, she cleaned the gash on Clay's head as gently as she could.

"Ow."

"I'm sorry, Clay-boy, I know that hurts. I'll make it feel all better in just a minute."

Ace had never been so relieved in his life as when he realized how calm and capable Belinda was. By the time she had the wound cleaned, Clay was down to an occasional sniffle, and Jason and Grant were dry-eyed and watching her every move.

When she came at Clay with a bottle of hydrogen peroxide and a cotton ball, Clay shrank back against Ace. "Is it gonna sting?" Clay asked.

"Would I do that to you?" she said, soaking the cotton ball. "It will just feel cool, that's all. Ready?"

Eyes wide and red from crying, Clay looked up at his father. For advice. For support.

Ace's throat thickened at the look on his middle son's face. He cleared his throat, then nodded. "It'll be okay. Aunt Binda wouldn't hurt you."

Clay swallowed hard, then looked at his aunt. "Okay. I'm ready." He scrunched up his face, squeezed his eyes shut and held his breath.

As she pressed the cotton ball gently against the wound, Jason and Grant scrunched up their own faces in empathy.

"You can open your eyes now." There was a hint of laughter in Belinda's voice, but her expression was suitably somber so as not to bruise a young man's ego.

Clay blinked his eyes open and smiled.

"Did it sting like fire?" Jason wanted to know. "Like that stuff Aunt Mary used?"

"Naw," Clay told him. If he'd been standing up, he'd have been swaggering with pride. "Didn't hurt a bit."

"Didn't hurt a bit," Grant mimicked.

Jack and Trey, standing almost far enough away to give Ace, Belinda and Clay a little breathing room, chuckled at Grant's comment.

Belinda put two strip bandages, each sporting a different cartoon character, in the shape of an X over Clay's cut. Then she brought a bag of frozen peas from the freezer. After placing a clean, dry hand towel over the bandages, she carefully placed the peas over it.

"Cold," Clay said with a giggle.

"Yeah. It'll make it feel better, and maybe keep

that goose egg from getting as big as an elephant egg.''

Clay giggled again, and his brothers joined him.

"How's your tummy?" Belinda asked the boy. "Are you sick?"

Clay frowned indignantly. "I hit my head, not my tummy."

"Can you see okay?"

Clay's eyes grew to the size of saucers. "You mean I could go blind?"

"No." Belinda smiled. "I just wondered if everything looked all fuzzy or anything."

"Naw."

"Okay, then. I think you'll live."

"You're pretty good at this," Ace told Belinda.

"You mean, unlike Cathy?" she said, a twinkle in her eye. "Don't give me that puckered-up look," she said to Ace. "I knew my sister a lot longer than you did. The least little bump or scratch and she got hysterical. I have to guess that if it was her own child who was hurt, she would have been about as useful as feathers on a mule."

Jason frowned. "What good's feathers on a mule?"

"My point exactly," she said, touching a fingertip to the end of his nose. "No use at all. Your mama just couldn't stand to see anybody hurt. Not that I like it much myself, but Clay-boy, here, is going to be just fine."

"So says Dr. Belinda," Ace said, his lips twitching.

"So says Hockey Player Belinda," she countered. "I've taken enough pucks in the head in my youth to know exactly how it feels to get a goose egg like this one. After a while, you learn not to get too excited about a little bump on the noggin.''

She gently ruffled Clay's hair. ''But I can't forget the most important medical treatment of all.''

Clay's eyes widened. ''What's that?''

''A kiss.'' She lifted the frozen peas and the towel beneath them, and placed a kiss on Clay's bump.

Then to Ace she said, ''Still, I imagine you'll want to have a doctor look at him.''

''That's where we're headed next,'' Ace said.

Ace and Belinda drove off a few minutes later with all three boys. Ace drove while Belinda held Clay in her lap and kept the frozen peas pressed to his head. After the visit to the hospital, they planned to stop off for ice cream. For medicinal purposes.

Jack watched them go and gave Trey a hearty slap on the back. ''Little brother, things are starting to look up around here.''

Trey slapped him back, grinning. ''Yeah. I think he's in heat.''

''And about damn time.''

''Amen to that. You think she can handle him?''

''With one arm tied behind her back. The question is, can he handle her?''

''Maybe not,'' Trey said with a grin. ''But it'll be a hell of a ride.''

Chapter Five

"Look right into the light." The doctor aimed his little penlight straight into Clay's eyes one at a time. "Did you get sick to your tummy?"

"How come everybody wants to know about my stomach?" Clay whined. "It was my head that went whack."

Dr. Carver flicked off his flashlight and looked up at Ace.

"I asked him that first thing. He was just as cranky then as he is now. But I don't think he was nauseated."

"Good." Will Carver loved working in this small-town hospital where he could get to know the people as people, not just as ailments on a chart. He smiled back down at Clay. "Do you remember what happened?"

"Yeah." Clay narrowed his eyes and glared at his older brother. "Jason shoved me."

"You shoved me first."

"Did not."

"Did, too."

"Boys." Ace stopped them with that single word.

Carver waited until the urge to laugh faded. "Okay. Jason shoved you. Then what happened?"

"I fell over and whacked my head on the fence."

"Steel post," Ace supplied.

"Yeah," Clay said, his eyes lighting up, grin spreading. "It made this really cool sound, like this big gong."

"Did you see stars?" the doctor asked.

"Naw," Clay said, obviously disappointed. Then he perked up. "But I heard that gong. Does that count?"

"I suppose," Will said, smiling. "Did you know where you were?"

"Well, sure." The look on Clay's face made it plain that he thought the question was stupid. "We was at the corral, watchin' Daddy ride Bingo."

"Did he lose consciousness?" he asked Ace.

"No."

The doctor took a final look at the X ray, then taped a thick gauze pad where Belinda's cartoon bandage strips had been. "You're a lucky young man, Mr. Wilder."

Clay scrunched up his face and looked at Ace. "Is he talkin' to you?"

The doctor laughed. "No, I meant you. You've got a big ol' knot on your head—"

"A goose egg," Clay supplied.

"Yes, a goose egg. And I imagine that within the

next day or two you're going to have one, if not two, great big shiners.''

"Really?" Clay asked hopefully.

"Just like a raccoon."

"Cool."

"Other than that," Carver said to Ace, "he'll be fine. To raise a knot that size, he had to have hit his head hard enough to cause a concussion, but with no other symptoms, it's a very mild one, if that. You'll want to keep an eye on him, keep him quiet. No rough play, no horseback rides for the next couple of days. Once that knot starts to go down, you can pretty much turn him loose." To Clay he said, "But don't go hitting your head on anything. If you think this one hurt, it'll be much, much worse the next time. So you be careful, okay?"

At the thought of a possible next time hurting worse, Clay's color faded. "Yes, sir," he said with a swallow.

To take the look of fear out of the boy's eyes, Carver handed out suckers all around.

As they got ready to leave the hospital, Clay looked up at Ace. "Can I have my ice cream now, Daddy, like you promised?"

His expression was so deliberately pitiful, it was all Ace and Belinda could do not to laugh.

But Ace knew that no matter how manipulative the expression, this middle son of his had taken a hard whack to the head and had to be hurting. And he *had* promised ice cream.

They went to Smiley's Burger Barn for hamburgers, followed by the promised ice cream. By the time they got home it was nearing dark and Clay was drooping in his seat. Ace carried him upstairs and got him bathed and in bed—where he fell instantly asleep—while Belinda kept Jason and Grant occupied downstairs. Once their baths were out of the way, Ace tucked them in, feeling extremely lucky that Clay's injury was minor, that he had three perfect sons.

Grant conked out the minute his head hit the pillow. Ace bent down to the lower bunk and brushed a kiss across his cheek.

"Dad?" Jason said from the upper bunk.

Ace straightened, and tugged the blanket up to Jason's chin. "Yeah?"

His eldest son looked at him with big damp eyes. "I didn't mean to hurt Clay."

"I know you didn't, son." He stroked his fingers along Jason's forehead and smoothed his hair back. "But when people fight, somebody generally gets hurt, even if you don't mean it."

Jason grimaced. "I guess I'll try not to fight with him anymore."

"I'm sure he'd appreciate that."

"I guess," Jason said with a heavy sigh, "I'll just have to stick with calling him names."

From the doorway, Ace heard a muffled squeak. He glanced over to find Belinda with a hand clapped across her mouth and laughter dancing in her eyes.

Planting his tongue against the inside of his cheek, Ace looked back at Jason. "We'll talk about it."

Jason rolled to his side, yawned and tucked his fist beneath his cheek. "Okay." His eyelids slid closed.

For Ace it was like seeing a switch flipped. The kid was out. After another moment of counting his blessings, he moved to the doorway and turned out the light.

"Don't you dare laugh," he told Belinda once they

were in the hall. "Neither one of his parents ever had an ornery streak like that. He gets it from his Aunt Binda."

"Yeah," she told him with a cheeky grin. "Right."

He followed her downstairs to the kitchen, where she poured herself a cup of coffee, then held the pot up and gave him a questioning look.

"Yes, please," he said to her unspoken offer.

She poured him a cup, and they both gravitated to the table, where they sat and sipped.

"Poor little guys," Belinda said. "It's been quite a day. Especially for Clay."

"Yeah, it has. I want to thank you."

"For what?"

First things first, he thought. "For staying."

She looked away quickly.

"For the way you handled Clay when I brought him in. You were good with him. A natural."

She shook her head and stared down into her coffee. "It was nothing."

"As the father of that little boy who was hurt and scared and crying, I beg to differ. It was everything."

She gave him a look of pure irritation. "Don't be nice to me, Slick. It's out of character for you."

"Most people think I'm a pretty nice guy."

"Humph. Good for them."

"I guess this means the lull is over, huh?"

"What lull is that?"

"The one where, for several hours today, you didn't seem to hate my guts."

"Why, Ace Wilder. If I didn't know better, I'd think you almost cared whether or not I hate your guts."

Ace closed his eyes and shook his head slowly in frustration. Damn stubborn, irritating woman.

"Besides." She took a sip of coffee and met his gaze with nothing more than a slight smile. "I don't hate your guts."

"Couldn't prove it by me," he muttered.

"I think we just rub each other the wrong way."

The first thing that popped into Ace's mind—that he'd sure like to rub her, all right, in several very right ways—shocked him so badly that he took a big gulp of coffee to drown the words, and got a scalded tongue for his efforts.

Maybe Elaine had been closer to the truth than he'd realized. Not that he needed a wife. He wasn't ready to even think of that yet, might not ever be. But a woman... Maybe that's all this meant—he'd been too long without a woman.

But when he decided he was ready to break his fast, it wouldn't be, couldn't be, with his wife's sister.

The clock beside Belinda's bed read 1:00 a.m. What had wakened her? A sound. A noise. She sat up and thought she heard the low murmur of a voice.

Clay? Was he all right? Was he still sleeping? How good was that Dr. Carver, anyway? Suppose the injury was worse than he'd thought. What if it was a concussion, a severe one?

You ninny. Now you sound like Cathy, panicking instead of thinking.

Okay, she wouldn't panic. She would think. And she'd think a whole lot better after she'd looked in on Clay.

Climbing out of bed, she eased her door open and tiptoed across the hall...and nearly screamed as a large shadow loomed up from beside Clay's bed across from the bunk beds. The form turned, and the meager glow of the night-light revealed Ace's face.

She let out a huff of breath and felt her heart slide back down into her chest where it belonged.

"Sorry," Ace said quietly. "Didn't mean to wake you."

She moved closer and looked down at Clay. "How is he?"

"He's okay. Cranky because I woke him."

"That's to be expected."

Ace's voice, when it came again, came as a low, ragged whisper. "He's so small."

Belinda turned, and the unguarded look on Ace's face brought an ache to her heart. He looked so alone, so lonely. She wanted, very badly, to reach out and touch him. To smooth the lines of uncertainty from his face with her fingers, her lips.

Of what, she wondered, was he uncertain? But she would not ask. He'd always seemed so sure of himself. Cocky with it. But not now. Now he looked as though he needed someone to cradle and comfort him, and she wished with all her heart that someone was her. She hoped that wish was not in her voice when she whispered his name.

"So small," he whispered again, gazing down at Clay.

The wish spread out from her heart, bypassed her head and settled in her fingers. She reached up and stroked his brow, his cheek.

For one shuddering moment of weakness, Ace turned his face into her hand. He'd known, at some level, that she had a generous heart. While he'd never expected any of that generosity to be directed at him, now that it was, he didn't have the strength to turn away from it. Just then, he needed…something. Comfort, he admitted, and just then he needed it so badly that he didn't care if that made him weak. He wanted to slip his arms around her, feel her slip hers around him, and just hold on. He wanted someone to share this incredible burden with. For a few minutes. Just a few minutes. Until he got his balance back.

"Belinda, I…"

"Shh." She pressed her fingertips to his lips, stilling whatever it was he'd been about to say. Then, as if reading his mind, she slipped her arms around his waist and rested her head against his shoulder. "Don't say anything."

He didn't. Couldn't. When was the last time a woman had held him, asking nothing, giving everything? He wrapped his arms around her shoulders and rested his cheek against the top of her head. His breath came out in a long, quiet sigh.

It wasn't the sigh so much as the quiet, trusting way he rested his cheek against her head that tore a hole through Belinda's heart and left it gaping. As truth rushed out and swamped her, pain washed in. Great big waves of it. She was in love with him.

With that realization, she understood so much about herself that she'd been denying for years. This, then, was the real reason she purposely kept him at a distance, deliberately irritated him. It was her unconscious defense mechanism against wanting something she could never have. Her sister's husband.

Of course, he wasn't her sister's husband any longer. Hadn't been for two years. Her head knew that. But it didn't make her feel any less like she was trying to snatch at something that by rights belonged to Cathy. Cathy's husband. Cathy's children.

In abject misery, she pulled away from Ace and stepped around him toward the door. "Good night."

Twice more during the night she heard Ace go in and check on Clay. Each time, she fisted her hands in the sheet and pulled the covers over her head, fighting the urge to run to him.

Ace wasn't sure he could face her the next morning. He stood outside his own back door, as he had only a few days ago, her first day there, trying to work up his nerve to walk into his own kitchen.

She shouldn't have felt so right in his arms. She shouldn't have offered him comfort.

He shouldn't have needed it. Hell, the boys were always getting scrapes and bumps. It was part of growing up. Jason had done worse to himself in the past than he'd done to Clay yesterday. While Ace hated to see any of his boys get hurt, yesterday's incident hadn't amounted to much in the overall scheme of child rearing. He should have been able to handle it better. Especially after his unkind thoughts of how Cathy would have fallen apart over that knot on Clay's forehead. She had been just too tenderhearted to be able to stand the sight of anyone—above all her own babies—in pain. That was nothing to be ashamed of. Definitely nothing for a husband to complain about.

But Belinda had handled the situation as though she'd been dealing with little boys' hurts all her life. And later, in the darkness of the boys' room, she'd handled *him* with the same warm compassion.

It didn't fit with the woman he knew. That, and his

own need for that compassion, for *her* compassion, her warmth, her tenderness, had him worried.

Just suck it up, Wilder. All he had to do was walk in there and act as if nothing had happened. Because nothing had.

If, when he finally forced himself into the house, he couldn't quite meet her gaze, well, he had a lot on his mind, that was all. They needed to gather the cattle and get them moved up into the mountains. There were fences to see to, horses to train...work to be done.

Not that Belinda would have noticed that he couldn't meet her gaze, because she couldn't bring herself to look him in the face. If he smirked or sneered or laughed at her for what she'd done last night, she thought, she would die. She would just curl right up into a little-bitty ball and croak.

Right after she murdered him.

Thank God the men came in for breakfast less than two minutes after Ace. And then, that afternoon it started raining. It came in a hard, steady downpour that kept the boys inside and the men—except for Frank, who happily worked his horses in the indoor arena—soaked and cursing. It didn't let up—neither the cursing, nor the rain—for six days. The mudroom finally earned its name. Belinda made everyone leave their muddy boots there before they were allowed to set foot in the kitchen.

The boys, of course, couldn't stay inside *all* the time. As they reminded her, they had to gather eggs.

"It's our *job,* Aunt Binda," Jason explained.

"We *gots* to do it," Clay said.

Clay had long since forgiven Jason for giving him

a knot on the head and two black eyes. They were back to being coconspirators.

"You gots to, huh?" she asked, her lips pursed.

"Gots to," Grant mimicked.

"Grant, my man." She scooped him up, then sat at the kitchen table with him on her lap. "Let's talk."

"Okay."

"Well, that's an improvement. At least you didn't just repeat my own words right back at me this time."

"Nope."

"Good. I know you can talk all on your own, but I sure don't hear you doing it much."

He frowned at her. "I talk."

"Yeah? What do you say?"

He raised his shoulders and flopped his hands out, palms up. "I dunno."

"You don't wanna get him started, Aunt Binda," Jason said sagely. "Uncle Trey says when Grant gets going, he chatters like a magpie and won't shut up."

Belinda eyed the boy on her lap. "Like a magpie, huh?"

Grant grinned. "Magpie."

"More like a mockingbird," she said. It was obvious she wasn't going to get him to string a sentence together anytime soon. "Okay, let's dig out the rain gear and go gather those eggs."

A chorus of yippees filled the room.

Later that afternoon Belinda answered the phone to a caller responding to the reworded ad for a housekeeper.

"Yes, the job is still open."

"The position of nanny?"

"It's a housekeeping position," Belinda stated,

knowing full well the ad was more than clear on what the job entailed. "Nanny is only part of the job."

"You mean I'd be expected to cook and clean, as well as look after the children?"

"That's right."

"Never mind."

Belinda was left listening to nothing more than a dial tone.

Dammit, there had to be a qualified person out there who wanted a good paying job and wasn't afraid to work. There just had to be. She couldn't stay here all summer, no matter what she'd promised her mother.

For the men, the rain slowed everything down. Rangeland and dirt roads turned to muck. Streams and creeks roared with all the runoff and inched up out of their banks. Cattle had to be watched, particularly the calves, to make sure they didn't fall in and get swept away. Each day meant more hours in the saddle than the day before. They packed the lunches Belinda made for them and ate in the saddle, under no more shelter from the rain than could be provided by the brim of a hat. Twice they had to pack their suppers as well.

Belinda watched Ace drag in later and later each night, trying to act as though he wasn't about to keel over with fatigue after nearly a week of fourteen-hour days in a cold, wet saddle.

Wishing she could do something to help him, and irritated with herself for the wish, she frowned. It was after nine and the boys were already in bed, and Ace was just now coming in.

"How much longer can you keep this up?" she

asked, concerned despite herself. Hell, who wouldn't be concerned? He looked like the walking dead.

Having left his muddy boots in the mudroom, Ace crossed to the coffeemaker and poured himself a cup. A muscle in his jaw flexed. "Don't start."

"Don't start what?"

"You were about to nag me about coming home for supper and letting the rest of the men do all the work."

Belinda blinked. "I was?"

He shot her a narrow-eyed look. "Weren't you?"

"No, as a matter of fact, I wasn't. You wanna talk about it?"

"Talk about what?"

She refilled her own cup and leaned back against the counter. "Is that what Cathy did when you had to put in these kinds of hours? Nag you to stop?"

Ace pressed his fingers into his eyes and rubbed. "Forget it."

She didn't want to forget it. She'd just had her first real inkling that maybe, just maybe, Cathy wasn't as perfect as Belinda had always thought.

Oh, and damn, that was disloyal. If Cathy wasn't perfect, Belinda didn't want to know, because it would mean there was no hope for the rest of the world.

"I've got some of that chili left," she offered. "Why don't I heat up a bowl for you?"

He eyed her suspiciously. "Now who's being nice and acting out of character? But then," he added softly, "it's not the first time you've been nice to me lately, is it?"

Belinda resisted the urge to press a hand to her stomach to still the sudden fluttering there, but there was nothing she could do about the heat that rose to her cheeks. He was talking about the night Clay was hurt, how she had turned to Ace and offered comfort, how he had accepted it.

"Watch it," she managed, her voice only slightly shaky. "I'll have to make you heat your own chili just to save my reputation."

One corner of his mouth curved up. "Don't worry. Your secret's safe with me."

"I don't have any secrets," she lied. She put down her coffee and took the covered bowl of leftover chili from the refrigerator. The chili the men had smacked their lips over, claiming they'd missed tasting the secret Randall family chili recipe during the past couple of years.

Now *there* was a secret. One that had stunned Belinda. Cathy had been the world's best cook. She'd gone in for gourmet, but she could cook plain meat and potatoes with the best of them. And chili from scratch. If Belinda's chili tasted just like Cathy's, as the men proclaimed, then Belinda hadn't known her sister quite as well as she'd thought. Since no one had apparently caught on, Belinda could only assume— with a secret smile—that Cathy had been just as careful as she had been to hide the cans deep in the trash where no one would spot them.

Belinda's grin widened. *Secret Randall family recipe, my hind end.*

"I get nervous when you smile like that."

Belinda laughed. "And well you should." She started dishing up a serving of chili into a smaller bowl for the microwave. "And well you should." She laughed again.

Ace topped off his coffee, then sat at the table. "You're in a rare mood these days."

"Got you worried?"

"Damn straight."

Belinda served him his chili, with leftover corn bread, and started to leave the kitchen. She wasn't running from Ace, she assured herself. Wasn't running from anything, except maybe the feelings he set to stirring inside her.

Ace saw her head for the door and suddenly knew he didn't want her to leave. It was crazy, he knew, but... "How are the boys?"

Belinda paused and turned back, unwilling to admit she'd been hoping he would give her a reason to stay. "They're fine. A little cabin fever because of the rain."

"Clay's head?"

She crossed back to the table and took a chair. "The swelling on his forehead is down to a small knot. He says it doesn't hurt, but there's a bruise."

Ace frowned down at his chili. "What about his black eyes?"

Belinda chuckled. "Blacker than ever. Jason says it makes Clay look like a pro football player with those black streaks beneath his eyes. And older brother is pea-green with envy."

"The little rascal."

"Both of them. I caught them talking about which would be better for making a good set of black eyes on Jason—their bedroom door or the bathtub."

Ace choked on a bite of corn bread.

"They decided on the bathtub."

"They what?"

"Easier to wash away the evidence in case there was blood."

"Good God." Ace closed his eyes and swallowed. It really wasn't funny. They obviously hadn't carried through with their plan or Belinda wouldn't be sitting there talking about it so calmly, as if discussing the weather. Her lips wouldn't be twitching.

But it really wasn't funny.

"Jason wanted to know how bad it was going to hurt, so they wanted to try it out on Grant first."

Ace braced his elbows on the table and covered his face with his hands, trying not to laugh. "I…" But when Belinda chuckled, his laughter broke loose. He howled until his eyes watered. It probably wasn't hysterically funny that two of his sons were plotting to bonk the youngest on the head, but there was no meanness in any of it, in any of them. It was a typical boyhood prank, and considering the week that Ace had just put in, with more of the same staring him in the face, he needed a good laugh.

Between his sons' plotting and their Aunt Binda's laundry skills—or lack thereof—Ace figured he just might be able to keep not only his sanity but his sense of humor, as well.

During the next couple of days his sense of humor came and it went.

It came when the rain finally stopped. The sun came out, and with it, three little boys streaked outside to play. While Belinda followed at a slower pace, they raced down to the barn, splashing through puddles, squishing gleefully through mud to see their dad.

Ace had spent the morning losing his sense of humor. He'd gone to town to argue with the oil company over where they wanted to sink their next well on Wilder property. Ace had learned years ago to accept the necessity of oil and gas wells on the Flying Ace. When the drilling had first started, oil and gas prices had been better than good. The wells had brought in much-needed money, what with the way beef prices kept dropping.

But now the price for a barrel of oil was so low it wasn't worth it to him to lose another acre of his pasture or rangeland. Not that he had a whole hell of a lot to say about it, since the oil company owned the mineral rights. Legally they could drill just about anyplace they pleased, including right under his damn bed. But now they wanted to sink a well in the middle of the hay field, and they were going to have a fight on their hands. If he lost his hay, he lost his ability to feed his cattle in the winter.

Yes, yes, they understood his qualms, they said, but surely he was exaggerating, and anyway, what harm could a little crude oil, or the salt water they would inject into the ground, do to his stupid hay, anyway? It was just grass, wasn't it?

Just grass.

He'd explained as carefully and as calmly as he could that grass was all they had, but that since they couldn't earn a living on grass, they put the grass into their cattle and sold the cattle.

"Hell, Riggs," Ace had told him. "We've always cooperated with you, and you've always done right by us. Don't go screwing up a good thing now."

"I'm not trying to screw up anything. I'm trying to drill for oil, dammit."

"Yeah, yeah. But you know good and well that if you show up out there at that hay field with a drilling rig, my brother Trey's gonna greet you with his shotgun. Then you'll have to call the sheriff, and I'll have to call the governor, and my sister will probably call the media. Hell, you do it while my sister-in-law is here, she'll probably put it on the Internet for the whole damn world—literally—to see.''

Riggs heaved a long, slow sigh. ''You're not threatening me, are you, Wilder?''

Ace's smile was grim. ''I wouldn't dream of it. No more than you're threatening my entire family, our way of life, our livelihood, our ability to earn a living.''

''All right, all right. Let me talk to our chief geologist again and see what we can come up with.''

Ace nodded. ''You do that. And I appreciate it.''

Remembering the discussion now, Ace jerked another fifty-pound feed sack out of the pickup bed and tossed it onto his shoulder. He turned to carry it into the feed room in the barn, and stopped cold.

For one blood-freezing second, he thought his sons had carried out their little plot to whack each other on the head. Logically, he knew it wasn't possible. It would take a day or two before the skin around their eyes turned black. Yesterday, according to Belinda, the boys had been fine.

Setting the feed sack down so that it leaned against his leg rather than lay in the mud, he glanced up at Belinda, who trailed along behind the boys. She wore jeans today, tight ones. Ace wished he hadn't noticed. She reached down and took something from her hip pocket and held it up for him a moment before slipping it back out of sight.

Ace bit the inside of his cheek. Unless he missed his guess, that was a woman's eyebrow pencil she'd held up. From the looks of his sons, she'd done a credible job with it, too.

"Hi Daddy." Jason beamed up at him.

"Hi there, slugger." He dragged his gaze away from where that eyebrow pencil had disappeared and looked down at his raccoon-striped son. "What's new?"

Jason frowned and propped his fists on his hips.

"Daddy, Daddy, look." Grant jumped up and down for attention. "Look at me, Daddy."

"Hey, pard, how ya doin'?"

"Daddy." Clay tugged on his arm. "Don't you notice anything?"

"Well…" Ace tugged on the brim of his hat, then scratched his jaw. "I noticed it quit raining."

"No, Daddy." Clay bent and swayed, his face tight with disgust.

"About us," Jason said. "Don't you notice anything about us?"

"I notice you all came out to see me, and I'm mighty glad. But…well, now, wait a minute. Now that you mention it, there is something different." Ace frowned and gave each boy a close look. "Yeah, there's something different, all right. I just can't put my finger on it."

"Dad-dy," Jason moaned.

"Just give me a minute," Ace said. "New clothes? Naw." He shook his head and looked again. "It's not haircuts, either, but… Well, I'll be. Would you look at that, Aunt Binda? Jason and Grant must have hit their heads just like Clay did. They've got black eyes just like his. Well, I'll be."

All three boys giggled and jumped up and down.

"Well, guess we better load you up in the truck

and head for the hospital. The doctor'll want to take X rays and poke around on your heads to make sure you're okay.''

"Then we can stop for ice cream on the way home," Jason stated.

Ace shook his head. "Sorry, son, not today. Won't have time."

"No ice cream?" Jason complained.

"Sorry. Just X rays. Maybe stitches."

Jason's face paled. "Stitches?"

"We'll have to see what the doctor says."

"But there's no blood," Jason protested. "Me and Grant don't gots any goose eggs or nothin'.''

"No goose eggs," Grant repeated, shaking his head.

"That may be," Ace said, struggling hard not to whoop with laughter. "But you never can tell about these things. Head injuries can be tricky. If you hit your head hard enough, you could be bleeding inside your skull. Might have to drill a hole in it."

"No, Daddy," Jason said earnestly. "We didn't hit our heads at all, honest. Aunt Binda, tell him we didn't hit our heads."

"But you made me promise," Belinda protested.

"You gotta tell him, Aunt Binda. I don't want no hole drilled in my skull."

"Well, I can't blame you there." Belinda paused a minute. Who would have thought, she wondered, that big, tough Ace Wilder had such a playful side to him? Oh, she'd seen how much he loved his sons. He showed it to them and to the world in countless ways. But she couldn't recall ever seeing him have fun with them, tease them this way. She was nothing if not eager to go along with him. To Jason she gave a nod, then spoke to Ace. "Okay. They didn't hit their heads. I'll swear to that."

Ace stroked his jaw with his thumb and forefinger. "They didn't, huh? The only other thing it could be is that they caught them from Clay, but I sure didn't know black eyes were contagious."

"That's it." Jason jumped up and down, and Clay and Grant followed suit. "We caught 'em from Clay."

"Oh, boy." Ace nudged his hat back a little. "If it's this bad, this fast, we better get you boys into bed and quarantine you before everybody on the ranch comes down with black eyes."

Jason must have seen something in Ace's face that gave him away, for he narrowed his eyes, then grinned. "Ah, Daddy, you're pullin' our leg. You know these black eyes are fake."

"Fake?" Ace straightened and blinked.

"Aunt Binda drew 'em on for us with her eye-bow pencil, didn't you, Aunt Binda?"

"You made me promise not to tell that. And it was an eye*brow* pencil."

"See, Daddy?" Grant rubbed a fist beneath his eye and smeared black all over his cheek and hand.

Ace gave up and broke out laughing.

Belinda laughed, too, but not before her heart gave a little lurch. That same little lurch that happened on those other rare occasions when Ace laughed.

Even though the rain had stopped, the hours, for the men, were still long. But at least they weren't as miserably cold and wet.

The streams and creeks still raged. Cattle had to be kept away, leaving a considerable number stranded on the wrong side of a stream. Ace could only be thankful that they had a few days to spare before they needed to gather the herd for the move to the high pasture. And he prayed, as he had every day since the rain began, that it wasn't snowing up in the pass.

If his late hours made him miss the time he was used to spending at night with the boys, the up side was less time around Belinda. One minute she was conspiring with the boys to make him laugh as he hadn't laughed in years. Then she was nice, warm, friendly.

But in the blink of an eye, the damn woman could aggravate the spines off a cactus. Where did she get off moving his recliner and not telling him? He hadn't noticed the move when he'd gone up to bed last night, but he'd found it easy enough when he'd come downstairs this morning in the dark. Nearly killed himself falling over it.

She'd heard the commotion, of course, and come running to see what had happened. Laughed her head off at him.

With a snarl Ace hefted his saddle and resisted the urge to rub at the bruise on his shin.

"What's got you in such a pleasant mood this morning?"

Ace settled the saddle squarely over the saddle blanket on his horse's back and sighed. Most men wouldn't come near him in the mood he was in, let alone taunt him. But then Jack wasn't most men. "Nothing," Ace bit out.

"Oh-ho. Do I detect another round in the mating ritual?"

Baffled, Ace turned and faced his half brother. "The *what?*"

With a smirk, Jack ran his hand along his own horse's back. "You heard me. Mating ritual. That thing you and Belinda do when you snipe at each other."

For a minute Ace had trouble finding his voice. "Good God," he finally said. "You are out of your everlovin' mind."

"Don't you wish," Jack taunted with a wicked grin. Jack, who seldom grinned. Then he turned back to his horse. "I think it's kinda cute, myself, the way the two of you tap dance around your hormones the way you do."

Somewhere in the back of his mind, Ace was aware that his mouth was hanging open; he just didn't seem to be able to do anything about it. Him? And the Wicked Witch of the West? The woman who blamed him for her sister's death?

The woman who held you late in the night when you needed holding?

"No way, man," he said fervently. "You've got it all wrong."

"It's about time, too. You've been alone long enough. And no disrespect intended," Jack said easily, "but I'm glad to see you've got a woman this time who'll stand toe-to-toe with you and give you a good run for your money instead of agreeing with you all the time and letting you have your way."

"You," Ace said, pointing his finger, "are obviously suffering from delusions of sanity." Realizing his finger was trembling, Ace jerked his hand down. "The woman detests me, and believe me, most of the time the feeling is mutual. And that's a hell of a thing to say about Cathy."

"Yeah." Jack snorted. "But true. You just keep on

lying to yourself about Belinda, bro. She'll have you roped and branded before you know what hit you.''

The shaking in Ace's hands made its way into his stomach. ''Get a grip, Jack.''

''Yes, sir,'' Jack said, leading his horse out of the barn and mounting up. ''There's enough sparks in the air when the two of you are together to light up the state. Ought to be a damn good show when the fuse hits the powder.''

Ace stared in shock as Jack rode off in the early-morning light. His brother had lost his mind. There was no other explanation.

''Come on, fella.'' Ace grasped the reins and led his own horse out of the barn. ''Let's go check cows. Cows are starting to sound damned intelligent after listening to Jack run off at the mouth.''

Ace started to lift his boot to the stirrup before he realized he hadn't buckled the cinch.

''Damn nosy brother,'' he muttered, setting to work. Imagine Jack thinking Ace was attracted to Belinda.

What about those flukes?

Flukes were nothing. They were just…flukes. He'd just been celibate too long. That was all.

And she damn sure wasn't attracted to him. She hated his guts.

She held you.

She did. She did that, all right, he remembered, looking back up the drive toward the house. Why did she do that after ripping into him the way she had the night before about getting Cathy pregnant a third time? She'd hated him that night, for sure. But when he'd needed her…

''She just felt sorry for me, that's all.'' And that rankled. He didn't want pity from her.

What do you what from her?

Oh, hell.

Chapter Six

The Flying Ace was a family operation and always had been. One of Ace's earliest memories was of being held in front of his father on horseback and working cattle. He couldn't have been more than two or three years old, because by the time he was four he had his own pony and rode alone.

He remembered his father telling him how *his* father, Earl Wilder, had propped *him* before him in the saddle and worked cattle.

Ace had done the same with his boys, but today would be the first time he'd taken all three of them at once, and the first time they would take an active role in gathering the herd for the move to the high pasture.

He wanted, badly, to take them on the drive, but they were way too young, he knew, to be in the saddle from dusk to dawn. On the one hand he was impatient for them to grow up so he could share with them what, even after all these years, was still a thrill to him. The pride in the accomplishment of raising a good herd of cattle, of tending them, of moving them up into the mountains for the summer, herding them back down in the fall, cutting the beef for sale from the stock to be wintered over. To share that with his sons....

On the other hand, they were growing so fast that mostly all he wanted to do was hold on to them and somehow make them stay babies and protect them, so they would never have to know hardship, loss, heartache.

But without the hardships, the losses, the heartaches, he admitted, there was nothing by which to judge the good times.

Aw, hell, who was he to be standing around philosophizing about life? He did well just to make it from one season to the next. One day to the next. And that's what he would keep doing, making it from one day to the next.

On this day he and his sons would gather some cattle.

"Hang on to the horn with both hands," Ace told Grant. "If a cow decides to wander off, this horse is going to cut out after it. If you're not holding on tight, you'll be left hanging in the air."

Riding beside him on the bay mare Frank had chosen for her, Belinda said, "Would it be better if Grant rode with me?"

Ace chuckled. "How good are you at holding on? That horse of yours will react the same way this one will. She's a cow horse, Slim."

Belinda pursed her lips. "You mean she could just cut and run, whether I tell her to or not?"

"That's a fact."

"Oh, goody."

Ace laughed again. "You don't have anything to worry about. You're a good enough rider to handle it."

"Oh, well, my stars," she drawled, patting her hand over her heart. "A compliment from the great Ace Wilder. I'm not sure my little ol' heart can stand it."

Ace resisted the urge to turn his head and look at her. "It's going to be a lonely little compliment, seeing as how there won't be any more like it, since you don't seem to appreciate them much."

"I never said I didn't appreciate compliments." She grinned, eyes twinkling. "It's just that you're so stingy with them."

"I wouldn't want your head to swell. You know you look good, on or off the horse. I had to send Trey out to the main herd so he'd quit drooling all over you."

Belinda turned her face into the breeze and closed her eyes, savoring the feel of the horse beneath her, the wind and sun on her face. She smiled. "Trey knows how to treat a woman."

Ace snorted. "It's like you say, if you ever told him yes, he'd run spitless the other way. He wouldn't know what to do with a woman like you, and you know it."

A little jitter of...something...made its way through Belinda's stomach. She opened her eyes and turned her head to look at Ace. He was staring straight ahead, and from his profile, she couldn't read his expression. "A woman like me?"

"Oh, no." He glanced at her out of the corner of one eye, but didn't turn his head. "You're not getting any more compliments out of me."

"There was some doubt in my mind that your answer would have been a compliment."

"Yes, sir." Jack grinned, nodding his head slowly. "Round three, in progress."

"Round three of what?" Belinda asked.

"I'm sure I have no idea," Ace muttered with a glare for his brother.

Jack chuckled and then let the subject go. He could stir the pot a little, he supposed, but just then he would rather concentrate on the feel of Clay's little arms hugging him from behind. God, what a feeling, having a kid hug you, depend on you and know you won't let him down. Jack envied Ace his three sons, and there was no getting around that fact. And he envied the boys, for they had a father who loved them, tucked them in at night, listened to them, held them, taught them, showed them by example—and a damn good one—how to be a man.

Jack shook his head at himself. It was old news that he hadn't known who his father was until he was twelve. Spilt milk, as they said.

"Uncle Jack," Clay complained. "I can't see back here. Your back's too big."

"Well come on up here, then." Jack twisted in the saddle and swung Clay around to sit on his thighs. The boy probably could have managed just fine riding his own pony, the way Jason was doing. But Ace wasn't taking any chances on letting the kid hit his head again when the bruises were still visible. Jack couldn't say he blamed him, either.

Up ahead of the three adult riders, Jason, on his spotted pony, flapped his rope in the air. "Get along there, cow. Move it on out. Hasten forward quickly, there."

Belinda clapped a hand over her mouth to hold back a burst of laughter. *Hasten forward quickly, there?* She chanced a glance at Ace and caught him grinning like the lone rooster locked in for the winter with a thousand hens. "Hasten forward?" she managed.

"I can't believe he remembered that," Ace said, shaking his head.

"Where on earth did he come up with it?"

"It's a direct quote from none other than Teddy Roosevelt."

"You're kidding."

"Nope. He was an Easterner, new to cattle country. That's just how he talked. At least until he got ribbed for it."

"Head 'em up," Jason called, waving his coiled rope in the air. "Move 'em out."

"Now that," Belinda said with a chuckle, "I recognize."

As she watched Jason herd the cattle and shout out his one-liners, Belinda's eyes misted over. *Look at him, acting so grown-up.* Imitating his father, the look of concentration on his face, the ease with which he sat his horse. God, he was growing up so fast.

"See that cow over there, Grant?" Ace pointed toward a cow in the middle of the dozen head he had purposely left for them to herd today. "The one with the white spot on her left flank?"

"Whassa fank?"

"Flank. Her rump. See there?"

"Dat one?" Grant pointed.

"That's the one. You'll want to keep your eye on her come next spring."

Grant craned his neck to look up at his father. "How come?"

"Because she only had one calf this year. Every other year, she throws twins."

"Twins? Like Tommy and Timmy Wilson?"

Ace laughed. "Yeah, like Tommy and Timmy, except these twins are calves."

"Is that good, Dad?" Clay asked from his perch on Jack's lap. "A cow that has twins?"

"You bet it is, if she can nurse them both so we don't have to bottle-feed one. Getting twins is like having an extra cow, but one you don't have to feed. Twice the production from a single cow."

Belinda smiled to herself. She knew that Ace didn't expect the boys to understand about production, beef prices and all that. But they would remember what he said, and come to understand the business of ranching that much sooner for having been exposed to it first-hand this way.

He was so good with his boys. Belinda's throat ached at the realization that Cathy would be pleased at how good a father Ace was, at how he was raising her sons.

What could be better, she thought, than a warm Wyoming morning, a clear blue Wyoming sky, and watching Ace Wilder teach his sons about cattle, about life.

As they topped a low rise and saw the rest of the

herd spread out before them, they all, without a conscious signal, drew to a halt.

"Golly," Jason said in awe. "Look at 'em all, Daddy. Are they all ours?"

Ace shifted in the saddle. "Every last one of them, son. There you have it—the Flying Ace Ranch, on the hoof."

It was, to Belinda's mind, an impressive sight, that huge shifting mass of black and red beasts, with riders coming in from all directions bringing more cattle to add to the herd.

Belinda turned to look behind, at the rangeland spread out to the south. It went on forever, it seemed. Stark. Beautiful. It rolled up into hills, which stretched into green mountains.

"Oh, look," she called softly. There on the crest of a hill to the west a herd of horses raced the wind. "Are they yours?"

"No," Ace said quietly. "They're wild."

The way his voice rolled over the word *wild* sent something primitive shivering down Belinda's spine. She knew, of course, that there were still small herds of wild mustangs roaming parts of the Rockies, but…to see them. To watch them run, with their tails flying out behind them, the sun gleaming on red, black, brown, white hides.

"No corrals for them," she murmured. "No saddles, no riders bouncing on their backs."

"No oats," Ace stated. "No sweet feed, no curry comb, no safety from predators, no warm barn in the winter."

Thoughtfully, sadly, Belinda turned her horse toward the cattle. "Freedom has its price, I suppose." And sometimes, like today, watching Ace teach his sons about life and cattle and ranching, she wondered if freedom and independence—hers—were worth the cost.

Things were changing. Belinda felt the shift inside herself, and it frightened her. She still got that jittery, vulnerable feeling whenever she was around Ace, but lately, particular today with him and the boys and Jack on horseback, she hadn't been able to find that deep core of anger that was her defense. The fear was still there, but more and more she found herself unable to come up with a pithy one-liner to maintain that distance between her and Ace.

And what was she doing about it? She was taking him a beer. Go figure. It was late, and he'd been buried under paperwork in his office since the boys had gone to bed. And she was about to say something to him that she didn't think she'd ever said before. It was probably a mistake, but it needed saying, so she would say it.

When she stepped into his office, he was turned away from her, scrolling through screens of spreadsheets on his computer. Reluctant to disturb him, she gave herself a minute to gather her nerve while she let her gaze roam the trophies, blue ribbons and huge, silver belt buckles in the crowded trophy cases along the wall behind the desk. Awards for Wilders going back at least three generations, awards for their cattle, for their horses, and one for a dog. There were county and state fair ribbons for pies, cakes, and breads baked by Betty Wilder, Ace's mother, and even, Belinda remembered with a smile, a couple with Cathy's name on them.

"You're looking exceptionally amused about something."

At the sound of Ace's voice, she chuckled and shook her head. "I was just thinking about Cathy winning those blue ribbons at the state fair for her pies. It sometimes startles me how different she and I were."

Ace's lips twitched. "Does this mean you don't plan to stick around till fall and enter your famous Randall-family-secret chili recipe at the fair?"

Belinda blinked. "You know. You've known all along."

"Guilty as charged."

"Why, you sneak."

"Me?" Ace protested, laughing. He didn't know what brought on this pleasant mood of hers she'd been in all day, but he liked it. It was a relief not to have to trade barbs with her for a change. "I'm not the one who carted those empty chili cans out and buried them in the trash. It seems," he added with a cheeky grin, "you and your sister aren't all that different, after all, in some respects."

Her smile turned sad. "Oh, yes, we are," she said, so softly that he barely heard her. "Different in every way there is."

The whirring hum of his computer suddenly seemed abnormally loud. Belinda's gray eyes were focused inward, looking at something Ace couldn't see. Though maybe, from the sadness lining her mouth, he didn't want to see. He'd never seen Belinda like this before. He couldn't keep himself from asking, "Meaning?"

Her gaze focused, and her lips smiled quickly. If

the smile didn't quite reach her eyes, and if that troubled him, he didn't have it in him just then to probe.

"Nothing," she said swiftly. "Here, I brought you a beer as a thank-you." She held the bottle out to him.

Ace reached for the beer. The bottle was frosty cold and slick with moisture, her fingers warm and soft. The contact of his fingers against hers shot a bolt of electricity up his arm and straight to his loins. His pulse kicked into a rapid triple beat. Ace jerked in response. Instinct told him to pull his hand away, but he could not. Involuntarily his gaze flew to hers.

Oh, damn. Her face was flushed, her eyes wide, her lips slightly parted. She felt it, too, that zap of awareness.

Ace thought again, Oh, damn. What the hell was going on here? This was impossible. Ridiculous.

And somewhere from the back of his mind came Jack's mocking voice: *Round four, bro.*

They might have stayed that way for minutes, hours. Ace couldn't tell. Finally he was able to take the beer from her hand, pull back and breathe. The instant the connection was severed, he told himself he had only imagined it.

He knew he lied.

"A, uh…" He stopped and cleared his throat. "A thank-you for what?"

Staggered by what had just happened, Belinda took a moment to realize what he was talking about. Then she told herself that her first instinct had been right—this was a mistake. But now it was too late, so she'd just have to live through it.

"For today," she finally said.

He sat back in his chair and tilted his head at an angle. "What about today?"

She shrugged, feeling more out of her element by the second. She needed to shore up the wall between them, not breach it this way. "For including me in what should have been a family thing."

Ace frowned. "But you are family. You're my sons' aunt. And it meant something to them, that you would go with us. Today was one of our annual rituals around here. I should be thanking you for going with us and making it special for the boys."

Now it was Belinda's turn to tilt her head. "You really mean that, don't you?"

"Of course I do. Why wouldn't I?"

She shrugged, fighting the sting of heat in her face. "No reason, I guess," she said, copping out. "Anyway, enjoy your beer. I'm going to turn in."

She made the second hastiest retreat in her life, second only to the night she had awakened in the recliner to feel him touching her arm.

If they didn't get some decent response from the ad for a housekeeper soon, she was going to scream. She had to get away from him. This was not supposed to happen. She was not supposed to feel things for him, things she had no business feeling, intimate things, hot things, yearning things.

She'd never seen a man back away from a woman so fast as he had from her just now, when he'd looked into her eyes and seen her reaction to his touch.

God, how humiliating.

Ace didn't like it. He didn't like having to admit to himself that maybe these weren't just flukes.

Maybe he really was attracted to Belinda. Sexually speaking.

What a daunting thought.

First, for God's sake, she was Cathy's sister. For some reason that made even the thought of anything developing between them feel appallingly wrong. Why the same thoughts about some other woman didn't seem to feel quite so much like he would be cheating on his wife he couldn't say, and he didn't bother to analyze. The fact was, no woman had interested him since Cathy. That it should be her sister who wakened him felt, quite simply, wrong.

And second, if he were looking for a woman—which he most definitely wasn't—it damn sure wouldn't be one who was more apt to bite his head off than to smile at him.

And *if* he was after doing something about ending his celibacy, he wouldn't be looking for anything more than physical relief. Belinda deserved better than that.

How noble, he thought irritably.

Okay, okay. He was attracted to Belinda. That didn't mean he had to do anything about it. He would just keep out of her way as much as possible, and everything would be fine. As long as they didn't accidentally touch. As long as he didn't have to see her in those damn skin-tight jeans. How did a person straddle a horse in jeans that tight, anyway?

Damn, don't think about straddling and Belinda in the same sentence.

Man, he must be in worse shape than he'd thought if something that innocent could speed up his pulse.

With his mind made up—again—to ignore the hormones that stirred to life around his sister-in-law, Ace left the next morning, along with all the other men except Frank, to drive the cattle up into the mountains. If he missed Belinda's sarcastic comments, missed seeing her throw breakfast on the table wearing those baggy sweats, missed hearing her laughter when she played with the boys...well, he didn't miss her. Wouldn't. It was his boys he missed, that was all.

And maybe his bed, he admitted as he pulled another stick out from beneath his bedroll the first night on the trail.

"What's the matter with you?" Trey grumbled from his bedroll five feet to Ace's left.

"Not a thing," Ace muttered. "Shut up and go to sleep."

They were camped in the pass, with the cattle bedded down for the night. Tomorrow afternoon they would reach the summer pasture, then start back. Without the herd, the ride home would go much faster.

"Ignore him, Trey," Jack grumbled from Ace's right. "He's just fighting his destiny." There was laughter in his voice with that last line.

"What destiny is that?" Trey asked.

"Would the two of you shut up so a man can get some sleep?" Ace demanded.

"Not for me to say," Jack answered Trey. "Except to warn you that you're about to be shot out of the saddle where Aunt Binda's concerned."

"What?" Trey sprang upright in his sleeping bag. "I thought you were just kidding about that. Ace and Belinda? I don't believe it."

"Good," Ace practically growled. "Because it's not true."

Jack hooted with laughter.

"Dammit, Jack, you're gonna spook the herd," Ace grumbled.

"Ace and Belinda?" Trey repeated. "No foolin'?"

"That's the way I see it," Jack said.

"That's because you've got your head up your—"

Ace was cut off by Trey's whoop of laughter. "Oh, God," Trey managed. "That's priceless." Another fit of laughter overtook him. It was several minutes before he could speak. "Ace and Belinda. Who would have thought."

"Nobody," Ace stated flatly. "Except an idiot who doesn't know what he's talking about."

"Ace and Belinda," Trey said again. "You know what I think?"

Ace pulled his hat over his face. "No, and nobody cares, either."

As if Ace hadn't spoken, Jack suggested, "That it sounds perfect?"

"Yeah," Trey said with a smile in his voice. "Perfect."

"Certifiable," Ace muttered. "Both of you. And dead wrong. There is absolutely nothing going on between Belinda and me, except that she's looking after the boys and the house."

"Only because you're not trying," Jack said with a laugh.

"Give it a rest. I am not interested in Belinda Randall. For God's sake, she's Cathy's sister."

"What the hell does that have to do with anything?" Trey wanted to know.

"Not a damn thing," Jack answered.

"Go to hell, both of you."

* * *

The men—except Frank, who wouldn't leave his beloved horses—were gone four days. Belinda thought that surely by the time they returned she would have herself and her reactions to Ace under better control.

She thought she was doing pretty well on that score during his absence. She concentrated on the boys and was able to thoroughly enjoy her time with them. Except for those times when they asked when their daddy would be home. Which was, oh, about every three minutes during that first day. It was better the second day, as they were occupied with giving Scooter a bath during the afternoon. That chore quite naturally turned into a water fight during which everyone, including Belinda, got soaked. Scooter rolled in the dirt and had to have a second bath that same day.

By the evening of the third day Belinda felt as though she had her balance back. She wasn't thinking of Ace every few minutes, and when she did think of him, she was able to do so objectively. More or less.

Just before bath time that evening, Belinda's mother phoned to visit with her grandsons. The boys were thrilled to talk to her. One at a time they told her about Scooter and the water fight, about herding the cattle, about their daddy being gone. "But that's okay," Jason told his grandma, "because Aunt Binda takes good care of us. She's cool."

That was, to Belinda, the highest of compliments. As near as she could tell, being considered "cool" put her right up there with Batman, Arnold Schwarzenegger and Scooter.

When the boys finished talking, Belinda took the phone and let them go back to watching television while she spoke with her mother for a few minutes.

"How are you feeling?" Belinda asked.

"Much better. I'm fine now."

"You sound tired," Belinda accused gently.

"Honestly. You and your father. You both sound like a couple of worrywarts."

"That's our job, Mom. Somebody's got to look after you, since you won't look after yourself."

"I am looking after myself just fine. And if I fall short, believe me, Howie is right here to straighten me out."

Belinda chuckled. "Hovering, is he?"

Elaine let out a good-natured groan. "Worse than a mother hen. But enough about me. How are you holding up, chasing after those three boys and their father?"

A tight knot formed in the pit of Belinda's stomach at the thought of her chasing after Ace. *Never!*

"The boys and I are getting along great." She told her mother about Clay's accident, the knot on his head, his black eyes, and her use of her eyebrow pencil to save the other two from like injuries. "We're down to plum eyeshadow now, heading toward green."

Elaine laughed so hard she got choked and started coughing, which told Belinda that her mother wasn't as well as she claimed.

"Oh, my," Elaine said when she got her breath back. "Those little devils, to try and fool Ace that way. Speaking of Ace, has he been seeing anyone?"

The knot in Belinda's stomach tightened. "Seeing anyone?"

"Yes, dear. As in dating?"

"I know what you meant," she said irritably. "When would he have time to date? He works from before dawn until dusk, then he goes into his office and works until all hours.''

''That's not good, dear. You should get him to take some time off, go to town, kick up his heels. He needs to get out more.''

''He's a big boy, Mom. He can take care of himself.''

''I know that, but I worry about him. He should be seeing other women by now. He should be thinking about getting married again. I said as much to him the last time we spoke.''

The thought of Ace getting remarried left Belinda feeling as if the floor had fallen away from beneath her feet. She wasn't sure what she said during the rest of the conversation. She wasn't sure what she did during the boys' baths, or when she finally put them to bed after their final half hour of television.

It shouldn't affect her this way, she knew. Of course he would want to get married again someday. Why wouldn't he? But when she tried to imagine it actually happening, his actually taking another wife, cold sweat broke out along Belinda's spine, and she felt more than slightly ill.

The entire time he'd been married to Cathy, Belinda had been fine. She had never even thought of the intimate details of their marriage. But that had been before she realized how she really felt about him. Now she feared that if she had to watch him marry another woman, she would be tormented with visions of Ace and his new wife tumbling across those navy sheets on his bed, when Belinda herself wanted to be the one—

Don't think about it.

But she dreamed about it that night. About being

stretched out beneath him in his bed, his hands and mouth all over her, hers all over him. The pounding heat, the searing pleasure. And then the dream changed, and there was another woman, faceless, in his arms, while Belinda was forced to stand aside and watch.

She woke in the middle of the night with tears streaming down her cheeks.

She refused to go back to sleep. The first part of the dream, when she and Ace had been making love, was too bittersweet to relive, for she knew it would never happen. Wasn't sure she would have the nerve to let it happen even if Ace…

The second part of the dream—the nightmare part—kept flashing through her mind until she grew so irritated she had to get up and mop the kitchen floor to chase it away.

Good God, she was mopping the floor at 4:00 a.m. because of a man.

How the mighty have fallen.

It was less than likely that if and when Ace re-married, Belinda would be a witness to it. While he might think to invite her—"You are family"—she would never attend. And she certainly wouldn't stand beside his bed and watch him and his new wife enjoy the physical aspect of their marriage. So why was she so upset?

Because you want him for yourself.

She rinsed the mop and flopped it back down on the floor. The idea didn't bear thinking about. Nothing was going to come of it. She was just suffering from an unexpected case of raging hormones, that was all. There was nothing special about Ace Wilder. Nothing at all.

Uh-huh. Just keep lying to yourself, girl.

"Oh, shut up."

She detested that little voice in the back of her head. The one that never lied, that wouldn't let her get away with anything. Where had the stupid voice been when she'd thought she was falling in love with Ace? Had it shouted out in her mind that she was an idiot? That she was delusional? That she was not in love with him?

The nagging little voice had been annoyingly silent on that subject.

Belinda refused to consider what that meant.

The more she refused it, the faster the mop swished across the floor. She would simply keep on denying these crazy feelings about Ace. That was the only thing she knew to do. The only thing that made any sense. She was no good at intimate relationships. Her marriage had taught her that much. If she'd failed to learn her lesson that time, it had hit home without question a couple of years later when she'd gotten involved with Gary.

Lesson number forty-seven in the game of life and love: never get personally involved with your banker. Moving several bank accounts when the relationship went up in flames—or, in her case, drizzled down to a trickle before fading away completely—was more hassle than any man was worth.

She couldn't even imagine how disastrous an affair with Ace would be. For both of them. He wanted peace in his home; Belinda was not a peaceful person. He would want a woman like Cathy, calm, quiet, content in the traditional female role she loved so much. Belinda was none of those things.

Cathy had wanted a man to lean on, to support her

and give her children, a nice home, security. Ace had been that man.

Belinda wasn't interested in leaning on any man. She could provide her own home, her own security. If sometimes her life seemed a little lonely, well, she had friends, didn't she? She didn't need a man in her life to feel fulfilled.

She stood back and leaned on the mop, shaking her head at herself. She had mopped more in the few weeks she'd been on the Flying Ace than in her entire life. She was pleased to realize she still hated doing it.

She rinsed out the mop and put it away in the mudroom, then put on a pot of coffee. No use going back to bed. Her mind was still sending out flashes of that damned dream.

God, she hated this. Hated feeling all itchy and helpless and frustrated.

"Enough," she told herself in the silence of the deserted kitchen. In the end it didn't matter how she felt about Ace; she wasn't going to act on those feelings. She wasn't about to make a fool of herself with him. Wasn't about to make herself even more vulnerable around him than she already felt.

By the time the sun came up, she had managed to work herself into a fine state of denial. She had blown things out of proportion, that was all. She was much too levelheaded to let a few isolated sparks get the best of her. That's all it had been, a few isolated sparks brought on by a long bout of celibacy.

The denial of any attraction to Ace, any soft feelings for him, grew in strength as the morning passed. She felt stronger for it, more in command of herself.

She was still nursing that denial when she heard Jason's shout from the backyard. "Daddy's back!"

Belinda was standing in the quiet kitchen, building sandwiches to go with the macaroni and cheese she'd just made for her and the boys' lunch. If her heart gave a little leap, it was only because the shout had startled her.

She heard the boys whoop and holler as they ran toward the barn to greet the riders. She caught herself turning toward the back door to follow them, then stopped. There was no need to go down and greet them. It was noon; they would be hungry and would soon be up at the house looking for lunch. She would just do the job she was here to do and put something together for them.

She had another pot of macaroni going on the stove when the back door opened. She turned more out of reflex than intent. And he was there.

Damn her pulse for leaping, her mouth for going dry, her hands for turning damp. Damn the room for becoming suddenly airless. Mud caked his boots and streaks of dirt covered his clothes. There was a tear in his left sleeve a few inches up from the cuff, and what looked like dried blood around the tear. His face was sunburned, and a four-day beard gave him the look of a desperado.

Her heart pounded. Never had she seen a more ruggedly handsome man. The sight of him quite literally took her breath away.

Those Wilder blue eyes locked on her like a hawk on a rabbit. She didn't much care for the analogy. When he started toward her with that slow saunter, her hands fisted. Liquid heat pooled low and deep.

He stopped a mere two feet from her. She could

feel his heat. Without taking his eyes off her, he picked up a sandwich and took a bite.

Neither of them had yet said a word.

Something in his eyes spoke of anger, and it appeared to be directed at her. Belinda bristled. He looked, she thought, like a man spoiling for a fight. Well, she had plenty of fight in her, if that's what he was after. In her current frame of mind, she'd be more than glad to accommodate him.

He started to take another bite of the sandwich, then stopped and tossed it onto the counter. Bracing a hand on the counter, he glared at her. "Flukes," he said.

"Actually," she said, "it's bologna and cheese."

"Cute. I'm talking about this." He reached out and grasped her hand.

Fire shot up her arm, down her body. In response, she jerked away.

"A fluke," he said.

"Whatever."

"It doesn't mean we're attracted to each other."

A shudder raced down her spine. "Of course not." If only she could look away from those eyes so intently focused on her, she could break whatever power he seemed to hold over her.

"I don't want you," he said bluntly.

Belinda narrowed her eyes. "Who asked you to?"

"And you don't want me."

Heat stung her cheeks. "You got that right."

"And even if we did want each other, we wouldn't do anything about it."

"Of course not."

"It would complicate things too much."

Over the sound of her own pulse in her ears she

could still hear the boys down at the barn. "Absolutely."

He stared at her another long moment, the muscle in his jaw flexing as he ground his teeth. "Damn." In a flash he pulled her to his chest.

Belinda couldn't even think straight enough to protest, before his mouth swooped down and took hers. Her gasp of surprise turned into a whimper of surrender as his arms surrounded her, his taste filled her, his heat melted her bones like wax put to the flame.

His kiss consumed her. It confounded, it elated. It devastated. She wasn't aware when her hands slid up his arms, over his shoulders, to clasp the back of his head and pull him closer.

Ace was aware of her every touch, her every breath, the feel of her in his arms. And even more, the feel of her arms around him. It was heaven, and it was hell, because it wasn't enough. Not nearly enough. He wanted to gobble her up in three quick bites, from head to toe. He wanted to bury his flesh in hers and feel her hot, slick welcome.

The thought made him groan. He pressed a hand to the base of her spine and pulled her flush against him. The sound that came from her throat told him she welcomed the thrust of his hips. It almost undid him then and there.

Gasping for breath, he tore his mouth from hers. "I can't—" To hell with it. Breathing wasn't all it was cracked up to be. Not when compared to kissing Belinda.

"Ace—"

"No." He took her mouth again. "Don't say anything," he managed without releasing her lips. She tasted dark and hot and exotic. She felt the same way in his arms. "I want—" He wanted everything. Right there in his kitchen.

"Yes," she said with a moan.

He bit down on her bottom lip and tugged, then dove in again. "No time," he said against her mouth. "The men…here…ten…minutes."

He knew he should let her go, but he couldn't. Not yet. He took, and she gave. Generously. All he could think was *yes*. This was right. This was good. And his control was about to explode into nonexistence.

But just one more taste of her….

"I'll just check and see if and when we're getting any lunch."

Jack's voice from just outside the back door broke them apart as nothing else could have.

They stared at each other, gasping, Ace's hands clutching her shoulders tight enough to bruise.

The back door opened.

"Gee." Jack grinned like a possum. "Am I interrupting anything?"

Chapter Seven

Lunch was a nightmare. The boys asked a million questions, which Ace did his best to answer. Jack didn't say anything, but whenever he got the chance, he would catch Ace's eye, or Belinda's, and wink. Trey caught him doing it and raised his brow in question. Jack merely grinned and nodded.

That seemed enough of an explanation for Trey. He ate the rest of his meal with a grin that matched Jack's for sheer audaciousness.

Belinda wanted to crawl into a hole and hide. For the rest of her life, maybe.

Ace wanted to hit something. Or someone. At Jack's interruption, he had reluctantly released Belinda and stepped away. While she finished putting lunch together he went upstairs and took a shower. A cold one. It didn't help. Except that he no longer smelled as if he'd been on a horse for four days. The wonder was that Belinda had let him near her, as rank as he'd been.

No, he thought now, glancing at her. The wonder was that she wanted him every bit as much as he wanted her. They could both deny it till the cows came home, but they would both be lying through their teeth.

So where did they go from here, he wondered. She was still Cathy's sister. That still shouldn't have anything to do with anything, but somehow it did. He still felt guilty.

For Belinda the guilt was worse. Not only had she practically devoured her sister's husband while standing in her sister's kitchen, but in some dark corner of her mind she still blamed him for his part in Cathy's death.

How could she want him? *How?*

No answer came from her mind or her heart. She only knew that she did want him, did care for him much more than she should.

Care for? Get real, girl.

Yeah, yeah, so it was more than that. But until she resolved things in her own mind, she wasn't about to even think that other, more accurate word again. She couldn't afford to. She would go crazy if she did.

Somehow she made it through the afternoon, past supper, and into the night. Her nerves were stretched taut, her skin felt too tight, and her pulse had yet to calm since he'd first touched her that afternoon. But she managed.

Now it was full dark. The men had gone their separate ways—probably to the bunkhouse for a few hands of poker. The boys were in bed. Belinda had seen Ace take a bottle of beer out onto the front porch and knew she had to go out there. She had to talk to him about what had happened and why it couldn't happen again.

The screen door squeaked as she pushed it open and stepped out into the dark night. Ace was seated on the steps, his elbows resting on his thighs, the bottle of beer dangling from his fingers.

"Come on out," he said quietly. "Have a seat. It's a nice night."

The low, intimate timbre of his voice made her shiver. "We need to talk, Ace."

He raised the bottle and took a pull of beer. "Do we?"

Belinda moved to the porch post beside the steps and leaned against it. "You know we do. About this afternoon."

Rather than look up at her, he stared out into the darkness. "Was there something there you didn't understand? Or are you going to deny what really happened?"

"It's a little hard to deny, wouldn't you say?"

"I don't know," he said. "Seems to me like we've both been doing a pretty good job up until today."

She followed his gaze off into the darkness, finding it easier than looking at his rugged profile in the dim glow of the living room lamp and the utility light behind the house. "It was a mistake. Wasn't it?"

"Probably a lulu," he admitted.

Her heart pounded so loud she feared he could hear the thunder of it. "It probably shouldn't happen again."

"Probably not." He took another swallow of beer. "But it will."

When her heart resumed its beating, Belinda let out

the breath she'd been holding. "Before it does, I need you to tell me something."

Now he looked up at her, and she wished he hadn't. "Tell you what?" he asked.

Belinda struggled for the right words, the ones she thought she had planned so carefully that now eluded her. "Are you aware," she asked tightly, "that I've blamed you for Cathy's death?"

Ace felt like he'd been sucker punched. His breath left him in a hiss. It was a long moment before he could draw another. "I figured as much, after what you said a couple of weeks ago."

"You said I didn't know what I was talking about. That whatever went on between you and Cathy was private and none of my business."

"I guess I said that, yeah."

"It's still none of my business, but I'm asking, anyway."

"What, exactly," he said cautiously, "are you asking?"

She was quiet for so long that he started to hope she had dropped the subject. But no such luck.

"I know the two of you said from the beginning that you wanted at least four children. But dammit, why did you get her pregnant that third time, when you knew there would most likely be serious complications?"

Ace took another swig of beer, then let his eyes fall shut. "I didn't."

As if the very air around her telegraphed her movements to him, he felt her stiffen. "You didn't get her pregnant?"

A bark of self-deprecating laughter escaped him. "Oh, I did that right enough. But not intentionally."

"What's that supposed to mean?"

"It means," he said tiredly, "that she neglected to tell me she'd gone off the Pill. Yes, I knew the doctors expected problems with the delivery when she carried Clay. Which is why, after he was born, I told her we didn't need any more children."

"You..." Belinda slid down the post and sat next to Ace on the steps. "What?"

"You heard me. We talked about it, and she agreed. Sure, before we were married we knew we wanted a big family. Four kids, at least. After Jason we were hoping for a girl, but Clay was so perfect we decided we didn't need a girl, after all. With the complications of his birth, we decided two kids were enough. We wouldn't have anymore. We agreed."

"You mean...Grant wasn't...planned?"

Ace felt his heart twist. "What do you want me to say? That I wish he'd never been born?"

"Of course not." For the first time since she'd brought up the subject, her voice softened. "Of course not, Ace. I'm just trying to understand why my sister died. If you agreed on no more children, why didn't you have a vasectomy so you couldn't get her pregnant again?"

"You think I didn't offer? She wouldn't hear of it. She said it wouldn't be fair. That if something ever happened to her, I might decide I wanted more children with another woman." He let out a harsh laugh. "Can you believe that? She was worried about what might happen with me and another woman."

"It sounds like Cathy. But it's hard to imagine," Belinda said quietly. "The two of you were perfect for each other. She was perfect for you."

"She wanted—said she wanted to go in and have

her tubes tied. But she kept putting it off. She was on the Pill. Or so she said.''

''You don't mean—''

''I do mean. I didn't know she'd stopped taking the Pill until she told me she was three months' pregnant.''

''But...*why?*''

Ace shook his head. ''She wanted more babies. I remember when Jason started walking, she started wanting another baby to hold. Not just wanting. Needing. That's what she said. That she *needed* another baby. She said once that she felt as though her reason for existing was to have babies. My babies,'' he added, his voice breaking.

The anger that rose to Belinda's throat shocked her. Anger at Cathy. To have been married to this man, to have two beautiful sons, and feel incomplete? What incredible...greed.

Then shame swamped her. Cathy had more than paid for the so-called crime of wanting another baby. Paid with her life.

Still, ''Why would she have risked her life, after the warnings with Clay? Why would she do such a thing?''

Ace shook his head. ''She wasn't concerned about problems. They warned her of problems when she had Clay, and there were none. So she just dismissed the possibility. Right up...until the end, she never believed anything would...go wrong. Never believed a word the doctor said. She had made up her mind, knew what she wanted, and that was that.''

''God,'' Belinda breathed.

''I'm surprised she didn't tell you all of this.''

Belinda shook her head. ''She just kept telling me

how excited both of you were about the new baby on the way, how much you both looked forward to it.''

His Adam's apple bobbed on a swallow. ''I was scared spitless from the minute she told me she was pregnant. I even—''

When he didn't go on, she prodded. ''You even?''

Ace closed his eyes and remembered the pain. ''When I found out from her doctor just how dangerous the pregnancy was, I suggested an abortion.''

''Oh, God.''

''Yeah.'' He let out a long breath. ''She wouldn't speak to me for a week. Wouldn't do anything but cry. She was making herself sick with crying until I gave in. And if I say that I'll never forgive myself for that, that I wished she'd had the abortion, that Grant had never been born, what kind of monster does that make me?''

''No.'' Belinda reached out and placed her hand on his knee. ''It doesn't make you any kind of monster to wish your wife was still alive.''

''Thank you for that.''

She started to slip her hand from his knee, but he placed his hand over hers and held it there.

''I can't believe you let me kiss you today, that you kissed me back, knowing what you thought I'd done.''

Belinda wished she had a logical answer for that, but nothing about their situation was logical. She let out an exaggerated sigh. ''Sometimes there's just no accounting for taste.''

''Ouch.'' He chuckled. ''Damn, Slim, you're kinda hard on a guy's ego.''

She smiled into the darkness. ''I figure your ego's strong enough to take it.''

They fell silent for a while, his hand on hers, listening to the night sounds, the crickets, the cicadas. Up in the hills a coyote howled.

Belinda shivered. "That's a lonely sound."

"One of the loneliest."

After another moment she asked, "Do you get lonely, Ace?"

"Sometimes. Yeah, sometimes."

"Is that what this…thing, whatever it is, between us is all about? Are we just trying to assuage our loneliness?"

"Is that wrong?"

"I don't know," she answered honestly. "I just wish…"

He squeezed her hand. "What do you wish?"

"You'll laugh."

"Maybe. So what? You laugh at me plenty."

"Maybe."

"So? What do you wish? I'll try not to laugh."

"You're a prince, Wilder, and that's a fact. I just wish you weren't my sister's husband. Okay, now you can laugh."

"Afraid I can't accommodate you. I'm not that big a hypocrite. Not when I've been walking around for weeks wishing like hell you weren't my wife's sister. We're a hell of a pair, Slim."

"What do we do about it? I know in my head that she's gone, but I still feel guilty for…"

"Yeah," he said quietly, squeezing her hand again. "Me, too."

"Which is silly," she added. "I mean, we're not talking about a lifetime commitment or anything. We're talking about two people who—"

Ace leaned closer, until his breath brushed her cheek.

Belinda held her breath as his lips touched hers, thinking surely that she had blown their last kiss all out of proportion. Nothing so simple as a kiss could have had the effect on her that she thought she remembered. Nothing could be that devastating, that powerful. Nothing…

Nothing, except the feel of his lips on hers. The tenderness, in sharp contrast with the heated attack on her senses that afternoon, proved just as devastating, just as powerful. His lips were soft, yet firm, and warm. They teased and tormented and promised more. They made her yearn for things she had no business wanting, such as a lifetime of kisses just like this.

His tongue traced the seam between her lips, parted them, dipped inside to taste and be tasted. There was nothing else, only this gentle, soul-stirring kiss, and his hand atop hers on his knee. Nothing more. And it was everything, and it made her want to weep.

Then his hand slid up her arm and brushed her breast, and it made her want to feel his weight against her body, to feel his flesh mate with hers. And she was falling, falling, gently, and he was there holding her when she felt the porch miraculously rise up to press against her back. Only when he pulled away and looked at her, let her breathe, did she realize she was lying on the wooden porch, with Ace leaning over her, making her head spin.

"Ace, I…"

"Shh." His lips nipped hers. "It's just a kiss." And again. "Just a kiss."

Maybe to him it was just a kiss. To Belinda it was

so very much more, this swirling of emotions, sensations, things she'd never felt before, with a hint of more if only she had the courage to reach out and grasp it. One by one, each of her ugly little insecurities tried to rear its head, and one by one Ace unknowingly kissed them away.

Around her the nighttime air was cool. The man pressed against her was warm, so warm. Denim brushed against denim with a soft sound. Cotton against cotton. Breath against breath.

Against her hip she felt a ridge of male flesh swell and harden. "Ace?"

"You're not surprised, are you? This—" he nudged himself against her hip "—is what you do to me."

A low moan escaped her. Reaching for courage and boldness she didn't know she had, finding it in his touch, his kiss, she took his hand in hers and pressed it over her heart for him to feel the pounding. "This," she whispered against his lips, "is what you do to me."

Ace felt her small breast and resented the T-shirt separating it from his touch. Taking her mouth with his, he ran his hand beneath her shirt until he touched her, flesh to flesh, hand to breast. And it still wasn't enough. With a groan, he tore his mouth from hers and took her nipple instead.

Belinda's gasp of breath, her startled cry of pleasure, the way she arched clear off the porch, tore holes in his carefully constructed control. Suddenly, instead of the gentle tasting he had planned, he was devouring her, suckling, grinding his erection against her hip.

Belinda reveled in his sudden fierceness. Cupping

his head in her hands, she held him to her breast, biting back a moan as his mouth pulled at invisible wires that she'd never known ran from her nipple to the heat that throbbed between her legs. If he stopped, she was sure she would simply shrivel up and die.

"I want you," he whispered against her breast. "I want you, Belinda."

She said the only thing possible in that moment. She said, "Yes."

Ace raised his head and looked at her. "Will you come upstairs with me?"

"Yes." Again, it was the only thing she could say. She wanted him too much to give any other answer.

Ace knelt beside her and lifted her in his arms. He didn't dare pause to kiss her on the way into the house or up the stairs, no matter how badly he wanted to. He was very much afraid that if he stopped, that would be as far as they got before he lost his head completely and took her there and then.

But he didn't trust his control to last long, so he carried her to the closest bedroom—hers. The room was dimly lit by the glow of the backyard utility light. Ace closed and locked the door, then lowered Belinda to the bed. Without breaking his hold, he lay down beside her.

"Now," he whispered, "where were we?"

She took his hand in hers. "I think," she whispered back, sliding his hand up beneath her T-shirt until his palm cupped her breast and took his breath away, "we were here."

With his hand on her breast, Ace kissed her slowly, thoroughly, and the heat between them built. He kissed his way down the side of her neck until, with her shirt pushed out of the way, his lips trailed up her breast to settle over her nipple.

Belinda's breath caught in her throat. Oh, the pleasure of it. She wanted it to go on and on, to never stop. She wanted to return the favor, and she wanted more.

While his mouth tormented her, she pulled her T-shirt off and dropped it to the floor, then found the hem of his T-shirt and slipped her hands beneath. With fingers splayed, she ran her palms up the smooth, hard contours of his back.

Ace shivered at her touch. It felt so good he was torn between shouting for joy and weeping in pleasure.

"Ace?"

He tensed. Had she changed her mind? He wasn't sure he would be able to bear it if she had. Slowly he raised his head and looked at her. "Belinda, I—"

"Take off your shirt," she whispered. "Then kiss me again."

He nearly shook with relief. Rising to his knees, he peeled his shirt off over his head and tossed it aside. Then he eased down, his belly to hers, and slowly, slowly, lowered himself until they touched, bare flesh to bare flesh, waist to shoulders.

It was heaven. Warm skin and soft sighs, with the teasing scent of talcum powder from somewhere in the room. Her breasts nestled against the crisp hair on his broad, muscled chest.

"Tell me you want me," he whispered.

Belinda swallowed. "I want you."

"Right here, right now. You and me." And he kissed her again. Thoroughly. Fiercely. With lips and tongue and teeth, while his hands roamed everywhere he could reach.

Belinda reveled in it, let herself be overwhelmed by him. Welcomed him as he slid into the cradle of her thighs. The weight of him, his heat, his taste—it all felt so right. Too right—as though if she didn't hold on tight he would disappear into thin air.

She held on tight. The need for him swelled up inside her until she felt raw with it. She wanted to urge him to hurry, to fill this gaping need, to merge his flesh with hers. But she couldn't speak without taking her mouth from his, and she couldn't. Just... couldn't.

The muscles in his arms were rock hard. His chest and back felt like velvet over contoured steel. She touched him, stroked him, raced her greedy hands over every inch of exposed flesh she could reach.

Her heart pounded in her ears. Her lungs labored for breath. When his hips flexed against her, she welcomed his thrust, urging him on. Her head was filled with him, as was her heart.

Ace had thought he wanted to go slow, to take all night with her, but she suddenly turned wild beneath him, responding to his touch as no other woman ever had. She went to his head faster than the most expensive Kentucky bourbon. When he opened the zipper on her jeans, his hand shook. No woman had ever made his hands shake before. Not ever.

His hand was hot against her belly, and Belinda moaned. Then he slid it down, down, until he was touching her where she most needed his touch, and she thought she might die from the sheer pleasure. "Ace," she said breathlessly.

His name on her lips drove him higher, made him

harder. The feel of her against his fingers, so hot, so slick. He slipped a finger inside, and she was tight and ready, and he couldn't wait another minute.

When he pulled his hand away, Belinda whimpered in protest. She had just enough presence of mind to realize that no man had ever made her whimper before. It was right that it was Ace.

Then he was tugging her jeans down her legs, and she couldn't wait to be free of them. Her skin felt too tight, too sensitive, the denim too rough. She needed to have him inside of her.

Ace looked into her eyes, which, in the dim light, looked huge and dark. And filled with want. That this strong-willed, vibrant woman would welcome him this way humbled him, made his chest swell. Made him feel ten feet tall, as if there was nothing in the world he couldn't do.

He reached for his zipper, but she moved his hands away and lowered it herself. Devastating. Without bothering to push his jeans down, she cupped him with both hands. If he hadn't already been on his knees, she would have brought him there with those cool, clever fingers. He hissed in a sharp breath, his entire body as rigid as the flesh she now held with one hand, while the other strayed below, killing him with pleasure.

Finally he was forced to push her hands away or see it all end then and there. He hadn't been this close to losing control since he'd been a teenager with rampaging hormones. He wasn't a teenager anymore, but he felt like one, just then, with her hands slipping away, reluctantly, it seemed.

He kicked his jeans aside and lowered himself to the welcoming cradle of her thighs.

"Now," he whispered.

"Yes." She reached for him. "Now."

He started to move, eager to feel her heat surround him. Then a thought whipped through his mind, and he stopped. And cursed. And rolled away.

"What?" Belinda cried. "Ace, what?"

With an arm across his eyes, Ace clenched his fists and fought for breath, for control. "No damn condom," he said between gritted teeth. "I can't believe I almost—damn."

Belinda swallowed. "It's not a problem, Ace."

As fast as lightning, Ace lowered his arm and turned his head toward her. "It's not?"

"It's not."

Something in her voice had him rolling to his side and touching her arm. "You're sure?"

She tried to smile, but it didn't work. "I'm sure."

"It's okay?"

"Unless you want to call this off," she whispered.

"No way, lady. Not if you don't mind that I didn't come dressed for the occasion."

She gave him a look, all the way to his toes and back, that scorched him, let him know how much she wanted him.

He rolled until he once again lay in the cradle of her thighs. And then he filled her, and she took him in to the hilt. For one long moment neither moved, neither breathed, while they savored this first joining. It was more, Ace feared, than a mere joining of flesh. A great deal more.

But then she moved beneath him, and he was lost. That last ounce of control burned to cinders and set him on fire. For her. For Belinda. Only Belinda. No woman had ever made him feel this way.

The heat and hunger took them as he thrust, pulled back, thrust again. And she met him, thrust for heart-stopping thrust, breath for lung-searing breath. Hotter. Harder. Faster. Higher. Until there was nothing left. No yesterday, no tomorrow. Only now. Only them. With strangled cries, they flew off the edge together.

It was a long time before either could think again. Or breathe. And they started over.

At 4:00 a.m. Ace sat on the edge of Belinda's bed and brushed a kiss across her cheek. He'd already showered and dressed.

"Ace?" she murmured.

"Shh." Her voice was full of sleep, and, he thought rather smugly, satisfaction. It made him want to crawl right back into bed with her. "You've got another half hour before your alarm goes off." He kissed her cheek again, but she turned her head and captured his lips with hers, softly, tenderly. Completely. With a groan he pulled away and said softly, "Go back to sleep, Slim."

She whispered his name again, and he would have sworn he felt his heart swell to fill his chest. When she curled up on her side, he eased from the bed and let himself out of her room.

He checked on the boys, found them fast asleep. Downstairs he put on a pot of coffee. In the mudroom he tugged on his boots and left the house. Halfway to the barn, he stopped. There was no hint of dawn yet. The moon had set, and millions of stars filled the sky.

For a moment his mind shut down and his feet refused to move as he remembered the incredible night he'd spent with Belinda. His wife's sister.

What was he supposed to do with all these feelings welling up inside? How was he supposed to live with the realization that he'd felt things last night with Belinda that he'd never felt before? How was he supposed to admit that her brand of loving—so generous, so exciting, sometimes even aggressive—left him feeling breathless and wanting more? And that no other woman had ever done that to him?

Not even Cathy.

It felt…disloyal. He had loved Cathy, and she had loved him. She'd been the sweetest, most loving wife imaginable. Kind and gentle, always agreeable, ever willing to please.

Now here he was, falling for a woman who was not only her sister, but her exact opposite in every way. Looks, temperament, even—and most devastating to him—her sexuality.

But Ace knew, as he stood there on his drive and stared up at the stars, that, for him, there was no turning back. He would find a way to let Cathy go while keeping the best of her memory. There was nothing else for him to do. Cathy was dead. He had to let her go. Because heaven help him, he wasn't ready to let Belinda go. He was afraid, very much afraid, that he was hooked.

When Belinda's alarm went off at four-thirty, she awoke, as usual, alone in her bed. The same as every morning on the Flying Ace.

But she wasn't the same. She had changed during the night, in Ace's arms. Loving him had changed her. The man himself, the way he'd treated her, the way he'd made love to her throughout the night, the way he'd held her, kissed her, the way he'd whispered her name in the dark. All those things had changed her.

But a few minutes later, standing under the pounding spray of the shower, she was forced to ask herself what, really, had changed.

Last night had been…glorious. That was the best word she could think of to describe what she and Ace had shared. She had no doubt that he had wanted her every bit as much as she had wanted him. Even now, after making love with him three times during the night, she wanted him still. Again. Would, she acknowledged, always want him.

There was no doubt now that she was in love with him.

God help her. Because she still felt as though she were stealing something from Cathy. The guilt—misplaced, she knew, but no less real—weighed more heavily on her shoulders now than it had the day before. Because now she had gone beyond merely coveting her sister's husband. Now she had lain with him. Slept with the man her sister had loved with all her heart. The father of her sister's sons.

Was it so terribly wrong to love him, to want more of him? How could something that had felt so incredibly right be wrong? For the first time in her life, Belinda realized that she was, at her core, a very sexual person. Two years of marriage to Todd hadn't taught her that. One night with Ace Wilder had.

Always before, with other men, Belinda had felt inadequate. Todd had certainly told her she was inadequate often enough. But then, Todd would have preferred Cathy, and they both knew it. Cathy had never known, though, that Todd had a serious thing for her. Belinda had more than once thanked God for that blessing. As far as Cathy had been concerned, Todd had been a fun date once or twice, but nothing more. It would have been too humiliating in the extreme if anyone other than Belinda and Todd had known that he had settled for Belinda because Cathy had married Ace and put herself beyond his reach.

And it didn't take a genius to realize that Belinda had always envied Cathy her pretty blond looks and the adoration that her looks and her sweet nature brought her. It was no great leap from there for Belinda to understand why she'd married Todd. He'd been Cathy's, even if Cathy hadn't known it. It had been a way, in Belinda's insecure mind, to grab something for herself that, had it not been for Ace, might have belonged to Cathy. A way for Belinda, or so she had undoubtedly thought somewhere in the back of her mind, to live a part of Cathy's life. To *be* Cathy.

It made her sick just to think about it.

And now, here she was, making love with, falling in love with, Cathy's husband.

And that, too, made her sick. Because in the end, Ace would not accept her as a substitute for Cathy any more than Todd had.

"Oh, my God." Belinda curled in upon herself and leaned against the shower wall. "What have I done?"

It was getting old, Ace thought. And ridiculous. This reluctance of his—okay, he could admit it—it was fear, ice-cold, knee-shaking fear. He was afraid to walk into his own kitchen and face Belinda. And he'd be damned if he would let the fear or memories of Cathy and the guilt they brought or anything else keep him from Belinda. Memories couldn't keep him warm at night. Belinda could. Belinda had. She was the present. Maybe even the future.

It was getting even older, he thought a minute later, to walk into his kitchen and have Belinda refuse to look him in the eye. He tried a gentle good-morning and got a quiet response, but not even so much as a glance.

The gallon jars of milk hit the counter with a dull thud. "Okay," he said as Belinda stirred and studied the huge kettle of oatmeal on the stove as if it held the cure for cancer. "Out with it, Belinda."

Outside in the cool dark of predawn, Jack heard Trey walk up beside him.

"What are you doing?" Trey asked, his voice low in deference to the quiet.

Jack frowned at the kitchen window. "I guess you'd call it spying."

Trey folded his arms across his chest and followed Jack's gaze through the window. Belinda and Ace were there in the kitchen. The tension between the two, the unhappiness, was palpable even out here on the drive. "Hell, what's their problem now?"

Jack shook his head. "Did you hear him in the barn when he was milking?"

"No. I just got here. What would I have heard?"

"Whistling," Jack said grimly.

Slowly Trey unfolded his arms and looked at Jack. "You're kidding me."

"I'm not."

This, Trey acknowledged, was more serious than he'd realized. "Ace hasn't whistled in…"

"More than two years," Jack supplied.

"Belinda."

"That's the way I figure it."

Trey frowned and looked back at the window. "He sure as hell isn't whistling now. What happened?"

Jack shook his head again. "The damn idiot's started thinking again."

"Meaning?"

"Meaning I've had about all this foolishness I can stand. Those two belong together."

"You got a plan?"

"Little brother, it's time for drastic measures."

Trey grinned. "Can I watch?"

"No. You have to baby-sit."

"Huh?"

"Come on," Ace said again. "Out with it."

Belinda allowed herself the luxury of closing her eyes, but only for an instant. She set the spoon on the spoon rest and turned to him. "Out with what?"

"For starters, why you wouldn't look at me just now?"

She swallowed and glanced away, then forced herself to look at him. Then she chickened out and said, "I don't know what you want me to say." For a minute she was afraid he was going to advance on her, but he merely braced a hand on the counter.

"How about how big a mistake we made last night, that it never should have happened, that it can't happen again because you're Cathy's sister and I'm Cathy's husband and it just isn't right."

Every word he spoke was a knife to her heart. She couldn't read his eyes. Any minute, all of her blood would be pooled at her feet and she would die right there on the spot. "Is that what you think?"

"No." He made a cutting motion with his hand.

"I'm done with that, dammit. I thought you were, too. But it's what you're thinking, isn't it? Cathy is dead. It's time you and I both learned to live with that, don't you think?"

Belinda swallowed. She couldn't say what needed to be said while looking at him. She stared instead at the window over the sink, where only her reflection stared back. Looking herself in the eye wasn't any easier. She stared at the sink. "How do we do that, Ace? How do either one of us stop remembering how beautiful she was, how wonderful, how...perfect?" *When we both know I'm none of those things?*

The silence that followed her question was broken by a derisive snort. "Hell," Jack said with disgust from the door to the mudroom. "Why stop with 're-membering'? Why don't the two of you just build a damn shrine right here in the kitchen?"

Ace's jaw flexed as he turned to face his half brother. "Butt out, Jack. This is none of your business."

"You're right," Jack snapped. "It's not. But I'm damn sick and tired of watching two people I care about, who are obviously perfect for each other, mess up their lives, so I'm making it my business."

"No," Ace said, flexing his fists at his sides, "you're not. Get out. Breakfast isn't ready yet."

Jack's eyes narrowed, his chest heaved. "I own thirteen and one-third percent of this house, and I'll get out when I'm damn good and ready. The two of you—"

"What the hell is going on?" Trey demanded as he came in the back door.

"Round five, I think," Jack said. "And they're both trying to duck out of the ring."

"Huh?"

"Never mind," Jack said. He crossed the room and took Ace and Belinda each by the arm. "You're in charge of breakfast, Trey. And the boys." He started hauling Ace and Belinda toward the door.

"Okay." Trey grinned. "Sure."

Ace dug in his heels. "Turn loose, Jack. We're not going anywhere with you."

"Fine by me," Jack said. "We can do this right here in front of everybody, if you want. But I've got some not-so-nice things to say about a certain martyr who used to live here, and I don't think you want me saying them in front of the men."

"I don't want you saying them at all."

"That's tough, big brother."

Chapter Eight

The sun was just coming up when Jack stopped his pickup at the gate to the family cemetery three miles from the house. Belinda sat sandwiched between the two men, her jaw clenched tight. She had always felt closer to Jack than any of the other Wilders, but she was going to have to kill him for this stunt.

"This isn't funny, Jack." Ace glared over Belinda's head at his brother.

"So who's laughing? Get out." Jack opened his door and, taking keys with him, stepped out.

When Ace and Belinda got out, Jack took each of them by the shoulder and led them through the gate and in among the dozen or more graves. The rising sun turned the granite headstones a deep rose.

The names on many of the headstones read like a Who's Who of Wyoming history. King and Betty Wilder were buried here, along with all the Wilders before them back to that first one, John, the English baron who won the land from a homesteader in a game of poker. That original owner, Jeremiah Conner, was buried here, too. John's wife, Elizabeth Comstock Wilder, and their son, Earl, King Wilder's father. Earl's wife, Susannah Thomas Wilder, lay next to her husband.

There were others buried here, too. Four of the graves were those of ranch hands who'd had nowhere else to go when they died. Ace had once quoted his father as saying, "They're ours, too. They have a right to be here. It's fitting."

Then there was the stranger's grave. No one knew who the man was that King Wilder had found dead, halfway between the house and the highway back when Ace was a boy. But King had figured that since the man had died on the Flying Ace, he should be buried there. From time to time, Belinda had been told, flowers mysteriously appeared on the grave. No one knew who brought them.

Then there was Cathy's grave. It was there that Jack led them. "Loving Wife and Mother," it said on the granite headstone.

"Take a look," Jack said.

Belinda folded her arms across her ribs. "We've seen it before, Jack."

"Yes, you have." Jack nodded. "But I don't think either of you paid attention. Allow me to be blunt."

"When were you ever anything else?" Ace muttered.

"Cathy," Jack said, pointing at her grave, "is dead. *You* are not. And as much as everyone loved Cathy, she was not the noble, selfless martyr the two of you make her out to be."

"That's enough, Jack. Come on." Ace took Belinda's arm. "Let's get out of here."

"That's right," Jack spat out. "Go deaf, dumb and blind when somebody dares to present you with the truth."

Bewildered, Belinda felt her stomach twist into one huge knot. "Why are you doing this?"

"Because it's time that you admitted the truth. Yes, she was beautiful, and she was wonderful. But, by God, she was not perfect. What she did, getting pregnant that third time—not to mention *how* she did it, by lying to her own husband—was the most selfish thing I think I've ever heard of."

"Jack," Belinda cried. "How can you say that? She gave her life for Grant."

"That's where you're wrong," Jack said harshly. "She didn't give anything, because she was too damn self-centered to give, and she was too egotistical to admit that some doctor might know more about her condition than she did. She wanted a baby, so to hell with the doctors, to hell with her husband's wishes, to hell with the possibility of leaving behind two grieving little boys. Let's give Cathy another baby. Never mind that having a third kid could leave the first two to grow up with no mother, leave her husband with no wife, you with no sister, your parents— To hell with how it might affect everyone around her for the rest of their lives, as long as she got what she wanted. And if you ask me, what she wanted was another person to be totally dependent on her. Another baby."

"Are you finished?" Ace ask quietly.

"Yeah, I'm finished. If the two of you are so stupid-blind about your own feelings for each other, if you can't see how right you are together, if you're going to let a dead woman stand between you, then as far as I'm concerned you deserve whatever happens to you.'' Resettling his hat on his head, Jack turned and strode back through the graves to the pickup.

Ace and Belinda stood there, unable to look at each other, unable to move.

They heard the pickup door slam, the engine turn over. Tires crunching gravel.

Tires? ''Dammit.'' Ace spun and raced for the gate. ''Jack!''

Jack gave him a short wave and drove off.

''That lousy son of a bitch.''

Belinda caught up with Ace and stared dumbfounded at the dust stirred up by Jack's departure. ''He left us here?''

Ace propped his hands low on his hips and ground his teeth. ''Looks that way.''

''That lousy son of a—'' Belinda echoed.

''He's going to die,'' Ace muttered. ''I'm going to string him up on the cottonwood in the front yard, and I'm not wasting new rope to do it.''

After several minutes Ace cursed again. ''Come on. We might as well start walking. It's three miles back to the house.''

And so they walked. After about five minutes they reached the point where the cemetery road met the ranch road that would take them back to the house.

''You wanna talk about it?'' Ace finally asked.

''No.''

Ace reached for her hand.

She pulled back. ''Don't.''

"Don't touch? Don't talk? What the hell's going on, Belinda?"

"That's right, gripe at me," she said irritably. "Jack's full of it. You know Cathy wasn't like that."

"I'd say he both exaggerated and oversimplified, yeah."

"Fine."

"Fine? What does that mean?"

"Nothing. I don't feel like talking just now."

"Well, excuse the hell out of me. Last night you turned me every way but loose, and today you don't want to look at me, don't want me to touch you, don't want to talk. That's just sh—"

"Please. At least be more original."

"Slim—"

"I hate it when you call me that."

His brows rose in surprise. "Why?"

"We both know the only reason you do it is to point out that I don't have Cathy's figure. I have to assume that since last night the thought has probably crossed your mind about a hundred times what a poor substitute I am for her. But don't flatter yourself into thinking you're the only man who's ever thought that."

Ace grabbed her by the hand and pulled her to an abrupt halt. "You wanna run that by me again?"

She jerked from his hold and started walking again. "Not particularly."

"Well that's just too damn bad." He grabbed her again, stopped her again. "Is that why you wouldn't look me in the eye this morning?" he demanded, incredulous. "Because you think I'm using you as some sort of substitute?"

"You wouldn't be the first," she told him. "I'm

not sure what that makes me, that I keep hooking up with Cathy's castoffs. Not that she cast you off on purpose, but the effect's the same. She left you, so here I come to take her place. I guess a psychiatrist would say I'm trying to live Cathy's life, trying to become her." She frowned, thoughtful. "There could be some truth to that, I suppose. I've always been envious."

"What," Ace managed through clenched teeth, "are you talking about?"

"What do you think I'm talking about? Hell, Ace, it's as plain as the nose on your face. Or my face, I should say. Cathy was beautiful, with her fair skin and pretty blond hair, that curvy figure, the sweet personality. People fawned over her our entire lives. Who wouldn't be envious?"

"Slim, if I didn't believe it was wrong for a man to hit a woman, I'd pop you right on that stubborn chin of yours. I have never heard anything so asinine in my whole damn life."

"I didn't say I was smart about it. I know it's stupid." She shrugged and looked away. "I guess I didn't realize just how pathetic I was until this morning, when I thought about…last night."

"Great." He threw his hands in the air. "Yesterday you didn't want to get involved with me because I was Cathy's husband. Now you're saying the only reason you *did* get involved with me is *because* I was Cathy's husband? That if I'd never been married to Cathy you wouldn't have wanted me? And who the hell said I was looking for a substitute for Cathy in the first place? Because I'll tell you straight out, Slim, I'm not."

"I told you not to call me that."

"No, you didn't. You just said you hated it. Dammit, Belinda, I've been calling you that for years, and since you're too thickheaded and too insecure to figure it out for yourself, I mean it as a compliment."

"Get off it, Ace. If you'll pardon the pun, I don't stack up to Cathy. You know it, I know it."

"You got that right, sister. Cathy never argued with me like you do. Except for that last time, about having another baby, she always agreed with me on everything, always let me make all the decisions, let me have my way."

Belinda frowned. "Sounds boring as hell, if you ask me."

"It wasn't boring. It was…peaceful."

Belinda snorted in disbelief. "If you say so."

"And she never felt the need to always get in the last word, unlike someone else I could name. And I liked that peacefulness."

"Then what the hell are you doing with me?" she cried.

As if a switch had been thrown, Ace's anger drained away. A look of wonder, of revelation, came across his face. His voice softened, his touch gentled. "Coming alive again."

"Oh my—" Belinda's voice cracked, her knees weakened.

"Thanks to you," he added.

She didn't know if she reached for him, or he reached for her, but suddenly she was in his arms and was kissing him as if it might be their last moment on earth.

"Ace," she breathed between kisses.

"You're not blond," he said against her lips, "or curvy or delicate." He devoured her mouth with his.

"You're vivid and striking." He kissed her again. "Slender and firm and sexy as hell." Again, he kissed her, hard, fast, then pushed her away and looked into her stormy gray eyes. "And dammit, it's not a contest. And we did not make love with each other last night—three times—because of anything to do with Cathy. We made love last night *in spite of* Cathy."

"Ace—"

"Say it."

Belinda closed her eyes. A low moan escaped her throat.

Ace squeezed her shoulders and gave her a small shake. "Say it."

She opened her eyes and met his gaze. With a deep breath, she said, "In spite of."

Ace pulled her close again and squeezed his eyes shut. "We have nothing to feel guilty about, either of us. We're not going to feel guilty. Okay?"

Belinda wrapped her arms around him and turned her face into his neck. "Okay."

Tension drained out of Ace. "Okay. Then there's just one other thing."

"What's that?"

"We never said good-morning."

Belinda raised her head and looked at him.

His look was somber, but determined, as if he faced a difficult task that he had vowed to accomplish. Slowly he lowered his head until their lips touched. "Good morning, Belinda."

Nerves twisted and emotions bubbled. Belinda knew that it was her own insecurities that had kept her from turning to him this morning when he'd walked into the kitchen. Now she was getting a second chance to start the day right. Vowing not to mess it up, she leaned into the kiss. "Good morning, Ace."

Ace welcomed her by taking the kiss deeper. When he pulled away, he gave her a slight smile. "For the record, I like the way you argue."

Belinda raised one eyebrow. "Yeah, it's real peaceful."

"I've had peace. It was great. I loved your sister. Part of me still does, you have to know that. She lives in our sons. That's why you love them so much, because you love her. As long as we remember her, she's still part of us."

Belinda closed her eyes and took a slow, deep breath. He could have talked all day without reminding her that Cathy was still a part of their lives, would always be a part of each of them. It didn't help her reconcile making love with Cathy's husband.

"But, Slim," Ace said, "she's gone. She's part of us, but she's not here, and she wouldn't want us to turn away from each other and be alone because of our memories of her."

One corner of Belinda's mouth curved up. "Are you sure about that?"

For a moment Ace looked startled, then he shrugged and shook his head. "No, I'm not. But she's gone. We're not hurting her by being together. We're not hurting anyone."

"Except maybe ourselves."

One corner of his mouth curved, to match hers, but there wasn't much humor in it. "At least you didn't say each other."

"No, but I thought it."

He shook his head again. "Damn, Slim, why do you look for trouble? Can't we just take it as it comes and see what happens? We can't go back to the way things were between us, before last night.''

"We could pretend it never happened.''

"In a pig's eye.''

"Well, that's certainly plain enough.''

"I hope so. I'm not about to go back to pretending I don't want you, and I'll be damned if I'll let you pretend you don't care.''

Belinda hugged herself and looked off into the distance. After last night, she didn't think she had the ability to act as if she didn't care. Her defenses were too weak. Her willpower had shattered.

"There's no going back, Belinda,'' he said quietly.

She forced herself to meet his gaze. What she saw there was sheer determination, strong enough to make her shiver in involuntary anticipation of whatever might come next between them. "No, I suppose not.''

He let out a hoot of sarcastic laughter. "I guess I'll never have to worry about my ego getting out of hand with you around.''

"I didn't become a different person just because I slept with you.''

"I didn't think you had. I wouldn't expect you to.''

"Besides, your ego doesn't need any help from me.''

This time, his brief smile held humor. "Probably not.'' Then he sobered. He stroked one finger along her cheek. "I don't want you to change. I like the way you speak your mind, the way you stand toe-to-toe with me and argue.''

Belinda smiled slowly. "Watch out, you might get more of it than you want.''

Ace laughed. Wrapping an arm around her shoulders and starting them again toward home, he said, "I'll chance it."

There was more that Ace wanted to say, but he figured they had both been as honest as they could for now. He needed time to come to grips with all that they'd said to each other.

He'd meant what he'd said, every word of it. But there was more inside him for this woman, he acknowledged. More than he had yet revealed even to himself. He needed to think about it, turn it over in his mind a few times. Study on it.

And, he thought grimly, he had to strangle Jack.

With Ace's arm still around Belinda, they walked at a good clip as the sun rose higher and the air warmed. Ace figured it took them just over forty minutes to get back to the house, once they started up the road.

"What do you have planned for the day?" he asked as they neared the ranch headquarters.

Belinda ran her tongue along the inside of her cheek. "Laundry."

Ace opened his mouth, saw the trap waiting to spring if he dared mention his pink shorts and clamped his lips shut. He hated doing laundry. If Belinda thought he was complaining about the way she did it, it would be just like her to leave his clothes out of the wash and let him fend for himself. All in all, he decided, there really wasn't anything wrong with pink underwear.

"What?" she asked. "No comment?"

"Not a word," he said with his best innocent look.

"Smart man."

"I try."

Then they looked at each other and smiled. Until

Ace spotted Jack's pickup beside the barn. He stopped. "There's a little something I've got to take care of," he told Belinda.

She heard Jack's voice from inside the barn and nodded. "I'll leave him to you. I have my own ways of getting even."

The look on her face had Ace almost feeling sorry for Jack. Almost.

"See you later," she said as she turned away toward the house.

"Yeah." He caught her hand and pulled her into his arms. "But give me a little something to tide me over."

"Here? With everybody watching?"

"Here." He nudged his lips against hers. "And nobody's watching." He kissed her slowly, deeply, and she kissed him back, her arms twining around his neck.

And he was wrong. Everybody was watching. Including the boys, who were at the corral with Trey. It was the whoops and catcalls from the men that broke Ace and Belinda apart.

Belinda blushed, but only for a moment. The sight of money changing hands doused whatever embarrassment she might have felt.

Ace released her and raised his hands in the air. "Just remember," he said, fighting laughter. "I had nothing to do with that. I didn't know they were all spying on us like a bunch of worthless yahoos." His voice rose on those last few words loud enough to carry. "I'm just as much a victim as you," he told Belinda.

"Yeah, right. See you later, buckaroo." With that, she turned and walked toward the corral to collect the boys and head for the house. She felt the eyes of every man on the ranch follow her every step of the way. Most particularly, she felt Ace's eyes.

He was right, she decided. There was no going back, for either of them. What she had to determine now was, How far forward did she want to go?

She also had to determine her method of getting even for the catcalls and that disgusting exchange of money. Bet on her—or against her—would they?

"Boys," she asked, ruffling Jason's black hair. "What do you want for lunch today?"

Sabotaging lunch would be too easy, Belinda decided. The men would be expecting that, and if there was anything Belinda despised, it was predictability. In anything but software. Software should be predictable. Revenge should not.

When the men came in for lunch, she schooled her face into her most innocent expression. It was all she could do to keep from laughing at the wary looks on their faces. They eyed the meat loaf as if they expected it to explode.

Hmm. Now there was an idea... She would file it away for future use.

Right now she was too busy enjoying their discomfort. It felt good to dwell on that rather than on what may or may not happen between her and Ace.

Lord, she was out of her mind to get involved with him, but short of packing up and heading home, she didn't see any way around it. It had already happened. She was involved with him. Up to her eyeballs, and then some.

It wasn't smart, and being smart was one of the few things Belinda felt she had going for her.

First, she would get through lunch. Then the mind-numbing chore of laundry.

Throughout lunch she deliberately kept her gaze from Ace's face. But she couldn't help but glance in his direction every few seconds. His mere presence drew her, pulled at her. And aroused her curiosity when she noticed that he kept flexing the knuckles of his right hand. Equally curious was the way Jack kept touching his jaw and wiggling it as if to make sure it still worked.

It didn't take a genius to realize that Ace must have punched Jack for hauling them out to the cemetery and leaving them there.

My hero.

She didn't know whether to laugh or knock their heads together for fighting like two unruly little boys.

About an hour after lunch the boys were out in the front yard practicing their roping—the dog was in hiding beneath the porch—when a cloud of dust boiled down the road from the highway toward the house, announcing a visitor.

Having just spilled liquid laundry detergent on her hands, Belinda stood at the kitchen sink trying to rinse the slimy stuff off and watched as a gray Oldsmobile pulled up near the back door.

Terrific. Company at the back door, and here she stood, water and soap dampening her clothes, and dishes from the noon meal still all over the counter.

Well, Belinda admitted, she'd never claimed to be a homemaker. But it rankled to know that Cathy would never have been caught like this.

A woman got out of the sedan. She was fortyish, average height, with short, auburn hair. She wore a calf-length denim skirt, a pale pink, short-sleeved designer T-shirt and white sandals.

Wiping her hands on a dish towel, Belinda stepped out the back door and greeted her. "Afternoon."

"Hi." The woman took in Belinda's bedraggled appearance in a swift glance. Her smile was mischievous and contagious. "I guess I caught you at a bad time."

Belinda's lips twitched. She plowed her fingers through her hair. "Not particularly. Around here I nearly always look like this."

"I'm Donna Harris. I'm here about the ad in the paper for housekeeper. I called this morning and spoke with a man named Trey. He said I should ask for Belinda."

A week ago Belinda would have leaped on this woman. A real, live applicant! A day ago she would have gushed and prayed that this was the right woman for the job. But now, after last night, plus the events of the morning, all she could do was stand there and stare, feeling her mouth go dry, as a cold, dark emptiness opened up inside her.

"Is she around?" the woman asked, her smile turning puzzled at Belinda's lack of response.

An applicant, Belinda thought. A possible housekeeper. Someone to take over so Belinda could go home and resume her old life.

It's what you wanted, she reminded herself, but her own voice inside her head sounded hollow.

"Miss?"

Belinda blinked to clear her mind. "I'm sorry. I'm Belinda. Please, come in."

It took less than five minutes for Belinda to know that Donna Harris was the perfect woman to keep

Ace's house and care for his sons. Belinda wanted to hate her for that, but it was impossible. The woman was completely, utterly likeable.

"How long were you in the restaurant business?" Belinda asked. They were sipping coffee at the kitchen table, instantly at ease with each other.

"That depends on what you mean by 'in the business,'" Donna said with a smile. She paused and blew on her coffee. "When I was twelve—"

Belinda jerked and sloshed her coffee. "You worked in a restaurant at twelve?"

The woman laughed. "No, although that would have been easier than what I did do."

Belinda gave her a sheepish smile. "I'm told I do okay when I keep my mouth shut. Please, go on."

Donna told her of being twelve when her mother died, leaving her with four younger brothers and a distraught, angry father to care for—angry because his wife died and left him to cope without her.

"You raised four brothers?"

"More or less. I think they did most of it on their own, despite my so-called help. But I cooked and cleaned and took care of the house, the laundry, all those traditional female chores, until gradually each boy got old enough to take on his share."

"Ah, I like the sound of that."

Donna Harris smiled. "Somehow I thought you would appreciate boys doing household chores."

"Appreciate it? I relish it. We're still working on making our own beds around here."

"The ad said the boys are young?"

"Jason is six, Clay—Clayton—is four and Grant is two."

Donna let out a low whistle. "And you're single,

no children of your own, and you're trying to cope with all of this?''

"*Trying* being the operative word, but we're managing." Actually, Belinda realized, they were managing quite well, even if she couldn't see herself doing all the work she'd been doing lately every day for the rest of her life.

Rest of her life? Whoa! Where had that thought come from?

Wherever, it could just go right back. She had no business thinking along those lines. One night of mad, passionate lovemaking did not a lifetime make. Nor did she want it to. She was only here until Ace found a new housekeeper.

Now, seated across the table was a woman who had experience with children, with all the cooking and cleaning and everything else that went with keeping a house, and she had experience managing employees. The latter might come in handy indeed in managing the men on this ranch. The woman was, in a word, perfect. All she lacked, as far as Belinda could see, was Ace's approval.

If Ace and the boys liked Donna Harris—and they would, Belinda knew they would—Belinda's time on the Flying Ace would come to an abrupt end. Which was exactly what she'd been wanting since the day she drove up that gravel road and left pavement and civilization behind. Now she would be able to pack up her car and head home, get back to the real world, back to her life.

Oh, God.

Down at the corral, Ace spotted the gray sedan parked beside the house. He didn't recognize the car.

Nor the woman, when she and Belinda stepped out of the house together a moment later. "Wonder who that is?" he asked no one in particular.

"Applicant," Trey answered from behind him.

Ace turned to face his younger brother. "Applicant for what?"

Trey rolled his eyes. "For the job you've been trying to fill for weeks. Housekeeper."

Trey said something else after that, but Ace didn't hear him. The word *housekeeper* buzzed around inside his head like an angry wasp looking for a way out of a closed jar.

"I took the call this morning. She sounded perfect to me. Told her to come on out and talk to Belinda."

That part of Ace that had recently started coming back to life, or maybe coming to life for the first time, took the blow and stumbled.

Housekeeper.

Dammit. Why now? Why today? He wasn't ready.

He knew he couldn't postpone hiring someone, if it was the right someone. But the minute he did, Belinda would leave. That was the plan from the beginning. She would stay until he found a new housekeeper.

Then she would leave.

The thought of her leaving dried out his mouth and dampened his palms inside his gloves. It made his stomach clench and his heart pound in an uneven rhythm. It opened a hole in his gut big enough to get lost in. And suddenly Ace knew that if Belinda left, that was exactly what would happen to him—he would be lost. He would lose himself.

She couldn't leave. He wouldn't let her. Couldn't.

She was too important to him. She was...God, she was everything.

But how was he going to convince her to stay?

Belinda watched Donna Harris drive away. Squaring her shoulders, she turned toward the barn, determined to find Ace right that minute and tell him what she'd done. If he didn't like it, that was just too bad.

She didn't have far to go. The man himself was advancing on her like a man with a purpose. His eyes were narrowed, his jaw clenched, his hands fisted at his sides.

So, he liked the way she spoke her mind and went toe-to-toe with him, did he? Well, the man was about to get exactly what he asked for.

He stopped ten feet away from her, on the dirt drive. His gloved fists flexed. So did his jaw.

Belinda's heart started pounding. He was already angry and she hadn't even spoken yet.

"Did you hire her?"

Belinda cleared her throat and hoped he didn't notice that her knees were shaking. "No."

His head gave a slight jerk backward, as if he'd taken a punch to the chin. "You didn't?"

"No."

"I heard she was perfect for the job."

Belinda's nerves stretched taut. God, had she made a mistake? Had she assumed too much? "She is."

Ace braced his fists on his hips. "And you didn't hire her?"

"I did not," she forced through her tight throat. To hell with assuming too much.

"Why?"

She took a deep breath and held it. "Because I'm not ready to leave."

Slowly Ace lowered his hands to his sides and unclenched his fists. *I'm not ready to leave.* His heartbeat evened out, then raced. "You're not?"

"Nope."

"Why not?"

"Because you and I have unfinished business."

Relief weakened Ace's knees. Too close. He'd come too close to losing her. "You're damn right we do." In three strides he'd yanked off his thick, leather work gloves and had her hauled against his chest, her feet dangling in the air. Four more, and they were inside the house, their mouths locked on each other's. He moved forward until her back was braced against the wall. With lips and teeth and tongue, with greedy hands, with his whole body, his whole being, he quite simply, completely, devoured her.

She devoured him right back.

Hot, sharp need exploded between them. It roared through his blood. He couldn't get enough of her, would never get enough of her, her taste, the feel of her arms around his neck.

He filled his hands with her, with every part of her he could reach, finally settling his palms against her backside and pulling her closer, harder against his hardness.

One of them moaned. Maybe both.

He edged his mouth from hers and worked his way along her jaw to her ear.

Belinda groaned in sheer pleasure.

Pleasure. What a mild word for such riotous feelings. There was a gnawing hunger deep inside her, a ravenous greed for more, for all, for everything he had to give. Her mind clouded with it, her body burned.

Voices, childish and filled with laughter, rang out in the backyard.

Belinda gasped. "The boys."

With an agonized groan, Ace pulled his mouth away. He pressed her head to his chest and held her tight, burying his lips against her hair. "I hear them."

Belinda shuddered against him, trying to draw a decent breath to clear her head.

Ace felt her shudder and held her tighter. He wanted to absorb her, claim her, keep her. Wanted to bury himself in her and never come out. The only thing stopping him was the sound of his sons outside.

"You were right," he managed as he steadied himself. "Unfinished business." He eased away and looked into her deep gray eyes and knew their business would never be finished. Not if he had anything to say about it. "Tonight," he told her.

Belinda read determination in his face, and something else she couldn't identify but that sent a thrill racing up her spine. "Tonight?"

Chapter Nine

For Belinda the rest of the day by turns flew and dragged. She couldn't believe she'd sent Donna Harris back to town with a lame story about the need for a housekeeper being postponed.

Hedged her bets there. She hadn't told the woman the job was *filled,* only that they weren't prepared to hire anyone quite as soon as they'd thought.

"God, what is wrong with me?" Belinda whispered to herself.

But the answer was simple. Ace. That's what was wrong with her. He'd gotten into her blood. She wasn't ready to walk away yet. And that terrified her.

But behind the fear something bright and shining beckoned her. Something powerful and frightening, the lure of which she couldn't resist.

That, too, was Ace. Ace, his sons, the ranch.

She wasn't ready to let go of any of them.

So she would just hang around awhile and see what happened. Ace had demonstrated quite graphically that afternoon that he wasn't ready for her to leave. So she would stay. For now. For a while.

Never had she felt the things Ace made her feel. Never had she wanted to become a part of another person. If she let herself think about it too much, she was afraid she might panic. But not thinking about it was impossible.

"How can I avoid thinking about a man when I'm folding his underwear?"

"Now those are words to warm a man's heart."

Standing at the kitchen table with clean laundry piled around her, Belinda looked up and saw Ace in the doorway to the mudroom. Her smiled widened.

He started toward her, then stopped. "Where are the boys?"

Her lips twitched. "They're on the front porch, staying clean. Or so the plan goes."

Ace took a deep breath, then let it out. "Just as well. I'm filthy. I'm going up for a shower."

Belinda looked him up and down, saw the dirt, the dried sweat, and a few other stains she'd just as soon not contemplate. "Sounds like a good idea."

His smile turned lethal. "Wanna join me?"

Belinda closed her eyes. The sudden picture of the two of them, wet and naked, warm water pounding down on them, made her breath catch and turned her knees to rubber. Sleek, slick flesh gliding over sleek, slick flesh. Steam rising.

"Slim?"

The nickname jarred her from the fantasy and reminded her that she still had insecurities to deal with. And supper. "You go ahead. By the time you finish, the men will be here expecting food instead of laundry on the table.''

''We're doomed.''

''It looks that way.''

''Be damned,'' he swore. ''There's always tonight.''

''Yes.'' A shiver of pure anticipation raised gooseflesh on her arms. ''Tonight.''

''If I live that long. I want you.''

Belinda looked down. ''The, ah…'' She, who prided herself on always saying what she thought, had to stop and clear her throat to get the words out past the ball of insecurity that threatened to close her throat. She raised her eyes. ''The feeling is mutual.''

Heat sparked in Ace's vivid blue eyes. ''Hold that thought, lady.''

She watched him disappear down the hall to the living room, heard him take the stairs two and a time. *Hold that thought.* She shook her head. As if she could hold any thought *but* him.

''So how was the applicant?'' Trey asked over supper.

Jack frowned over his pork chop. ''Applicant?''

''For housekeeper,'' Trey explained. ''I took the call this morning while the three of you were out joyriding. A woman named Harris. Sounded good. Told her to come on out and talk to Belinda.''

Belinda concentrated on cutting up Grant's pork chop, while Ace did the same for Clay.

''What's a ap'icant?'' Jason asked, his meat already cut and disappearing as fast as he could chew.

When neither Ace nor Belinda answered him, Trey did.

"An applicant is somebody asking for a job."

"Oh." With his mouth full, Jason asked, "What job?"

"Don't talk with your mouth full," Belinda said automatically.

"Yes, Mother," Trey said, with his mouth full.

"Jerk," Belinda muttered under her breath.

"And Aunt Binda and Daddy Ace are both evading the question," Trey said. "How was she?" He looked at Ace.

Ace shrugged. "I didn't meet her."

"She was fine," Belinda said.

"Jeez," Trey complained. "Getting anything out of you is like pulling hens' teeth."

Clay frowned. "Do hens have teeth?"

"No, silly," Jason claimed. "It's just a 'spression."

"Oh. Like 'cold as a well-digger's—'"

"Yes," Belinda said hurriedly to forestall the rest of the saying. "But you shouldn't be saying things like that." She gave all the men at the table a dark look. Maybe Ace was right. These boys did need a woman around to help soften the edges some.

"Are you gonna answer or not?" Trey prodded Belinda with a glint in his eye.

Irritation, and uncertainty over the wisdom of her decision that afternoon, tightened her voice. "What, precisely, is your question?"

"Did you hire Mrs. Harris?"

"I did not."

"Why the he— heck not?"

Belinda widened her eyes in mock innocence. "It's not up to me to hire Ace's housekeeper. I'm not the one who has to live with her."

Trey looked at Jack. "What do you think?"

"I think," Jack said, "that nobody wants to tell you what you want to know."

"Yeah, that's what I think, too. What I'm wondering," Trey mused, "is why."

"Oh, for crying out loud." Belinda finished cutting Grant's meat. "You don't expect Ace to hire the first applicant—what is it you'd say?—right out of the chute?"

"After all this time," Trey said, "it looks like she might be the only applicant he's going to get. Seems to me—"

"Seems to me," Ace finally said quietly, breaking his silence without looking up from his plate, "that everybody would be better off minding their own business instead of worrying about mine."

"Well, pardon me," Trey exclaimed. "Until Belinda got here we all did double duty around this place because so much of your time had to be spent at the house."

"That was weeks ago," Ace said tightly, "and I appreciate all the extra work everybody took on to help me out." Damn his little brother, Ace thought grimly. If Trey kept pushing, no telling how Belinda might react. The last thing Ace wanted was for her to change her mind and decide he needed to hire the Harris woman so Belinda could go home and get away from his buttinsky brothers. First Jack this morning, now Trey was sticking his nose in.

"You're not having to take up the slack for me now, haven't had to in the past few weeks. That's all you need to worry about, bro."

Trey raised his brow at Jack. "I guess that means Belinda is staying."

"Yippee!" Jason crowed. "Aunt Binda's staying!"

"Now hold on," Belinda said quickly. "I don't want anybody getting the wrong idea—"

"Let it be," Ace told her, his voice low and quiet beneath Clay's and Grant's echoes. "Everybody's already got ideas. I've got a few of my own, and they don't include inviting the first stranger that comes along to move into my house and take charge of my sons."

Trey obviously didn't know when to stop. "Is that so?"

None of the men at the table, Belinda noticed, made any pretense of not paying attention to what was going on. It was a conspiracy, she decided, between Jack and Trey. All evidence pointed to the fact that the two brothers thought Belinda should stay. Jack had been so blunt as to give her and Ace a hard shove toward each other that very morning.

Matchmakers, she decided, were a pain in the butt.

"That's so," came Ace's laconic reply.

"Then maybe," Trey said with obvious relish, "you oughta take that ad out of the paper."

"Maybe," Ace said cooly, "you oughta go soak your head. How's the hay looking?"

In the blink of an eye, Trey turned from razzing to business. "It looks good. That rain we had right before we took the cattle up to high pasture really gave it a boost. You hear any more from the oil company?"

"Not since I told them you'd protect your crops with your shotgun if they tried to drill there."

"Damn right I would."

It was amazing, Belinda thought, that little Grant

could remain completely silent until a swear word caught his ears.

"Damn right," he parroted.

"Grant," she said. "You know you're not supposed to swear."

"Unca Tway did."

Clay took up the cause. "Daddy does."

Belinda ran her tongue along the inside of her cheek and gave both men a hard look while the other men decided it was time to study their plates before they broke out laughing.

"I'll tell you what," she offered the boys. "When you're as tall as your daddy, you can swear all you want, and I won't say a word."

"Honest?" Jason's eyes got big.

Belinda could read the little rascal like a book. He knew he was growing fast. All three of them seemed to get taller every night while they slept. He undoubtedly thought he would keep growing fast and be as tall as Ace in no time.

"Honest. As long as it's all right with your dad."

"Is it, Dad? Can we really swear when we're as tall as you?"

Ace eyed the eager expressions on his sons' faces and bit back a grin. Hell of a deal. "I don't see why not."

"And we can say hell and damn and—"

"When you're as tall as I am, you can say all those things. But not until then. Deal?"

Clay and Grant looked to Jason.

Jason gave his father a shrewd look. "Does that mean you can't swear, either, until we're as tall as you are?"

"Nope. I'm already as tall as I am, so I get to swear."

Jason's shoulders slumped.

"Nice try, kid," Belinda said, smiling. "But in the meantime, how about nobody swears at the dinner table."

"You realize, of course—"

The boys were in bed. The house was quiet. Belinda stood over the sink, drying the glass coffee carafe. At the sound of Ace's voice directly behind her, she shrieked and nearly dropped the carafe into the sink.

"Hmm." He gripped her shoulders from behind and started massaging. "Interesting. You're all tense."

"No kidding." Her heart took a minute to settle back down into her chest. "You scared the daylights out of me." His hands dug deep and found the knots in her muscles. Blindly she set the carafe aside and slumped over the sink. "Oh, that feels good."

Ace leaned close until his breath warmed her neck. His lips brushed her earlobe, raising gooseflesh down her spine. "I can think of something else that'll feel even better."

"Braggart."

"It would be a joint effort."

"Would it, now."

"Umm-hmm." He nibbled on her ear. "I make you feel good, you make me feel good, everybody's happy."

Her head tilted to the side, giving him better access to her ear, her neck. "Happy?"

"Happy." He turned her until she faced him, and

looked down into her eyes. "You made me happy at supper."

Her neck was limp. "Pork chops make you happy?"

He smiled. "I mean when you told the boys you wouldn't say anything about their swearing once they were as tall as I am."

She eyed him skeptically. "That made you happy?"

"It sounded like you meant to still be around when they grew up."

A new thread of tension wound its way across Belinda's shoulders, undoing the benefits of the massage. She hadn't realized her words might be taken as a promise that she would always be here. Oh, she knew she would always stay close to her nephews, but from the look on Ace's face, that wasn't precisely what he meant. A lump of nerves lodged in her throat.

"That made me happy," he said.

"Ace—"

"I want you to stay," he told her. "This afternoon, when I thought you'd hired that woman and that you might leave, I knew I couldn't let you go. You belong here. With me. Always."

It was the words *belong* and *always* that terrified her. Dried out the inside of her mouth.

"I love you, Belinda. If you're honest, you'll admit you love me, too."

"I never said—"

"You did, in a dozen ways. Do you think I don't know that if you weren't in love with me you wouldn't have let me touch you last night?"

"Ace, I—"

"Marry me."

Oh, God. This was the last thing she had expected from him. Her mind went blank. Just…blank. Then it started scrambling around like a starving mouse in search of the cheese hidden on the other side of the maze. Darting here and there, running into solid walls. Backtracking. More walls.

Marriage. Good God. Perhaps if she hadn't been so overwhelmed by what was happening between her and Ace she might have realized… But she had been overwhelmed. Was still overwhelmed. She'd thought only as far as not being ready to let him hire a housekeeper. Somewhere in the back of her mind maybe she'd been thinking she would stay through the summer.

But marriage? Marriage was for a lifetime. Or, it was supposed to be. She'd tried it once and had failed. Miserably. Marriage was for accommodating, domestic types. Like Cathy. Like her mother. Born homemakers. Women who didn't mind having a man to answer to for every little thing.

Belinda needed her independence. The freedom to come and go as she pleased with no one to answer to, no one to worry about but herself. No one pushing and prodding at her deepest pain, her darkest secrets.

"You look," Ace said tersely, "like I just asked you to slit your wrists."

"Close enough," she whispered.

"Come on," he said, cajoling. "You don't mean that."

"I do." She shook her head. "I'm…flattered. More than flattered that you asked, but I can't marry you, Ace."

"You mean won't." He stepped back and dropped his arms to his sides. "Mind telling me why?"

That old, defensive anger that used to come in so handy seemed to have deserted her. She had to struggle to speak at all. "Get real," she said with a small, harsh laugh. "Think who you're asking, Ace. This is me, remember? I know you said you get a kick out of arguing with me, but you don't want a lifetime of that, and I won't change for you. I don't know how to change myself."

"I didn't ask you to change," he said earnestly. "I don't expect you to, wouldn't want you to. I told you that this morning."

"I've been married, Ace."

"So have I."

"Yes, but look at the difference," she cried. "Your marriage worked. It was wonderful. Mine was a disaster. I don't want that for us."

"What do you want for us?" he asked tightly. "A summer fling?"

His words stung. She hadn't thought about the future at all. Now she was paying for her deliberate evasion.

"Damnation," he cried. "That is what you want, isn't it? You wanna shack up for the summer, play a little slap and tickle, then hop in your little red car and zip on back to your real life, so long, sucker."

"No,' she cried. "You make it sound...ugly. That isn't what I want. It doesn't have to be that way."

"Damn right it doesn't. We can get married and live as husband and wife."

"We don't have to get married to be together," she said desperately. "Why can't we just keep on the way we are?"

"That's good enough for you? Tiptoeing down the hall to each other's room after the boys are asleep, hoping one of them doesn't wake up in the middle of the night and come looking for one of us? Letting everyone in three counties speculate on that hot sister-in-law Ace Wilder's shacking up with? Letting them call you names? Is that how you want it?''

A deep chill settled in Belinda's bones. Was he hurting her this way on purpose? She folded her arms across her chest in a futile attempt to get warm. ''You know it isn't. You're exaggerating. Why should anyone but you and me care what we do?''

''Look around you, Slim. This isn't Denver. But then, maybe that's part of the problem. Maybe it's too isolated for you out here in the middle of nowhere.''

''That has nothing to do with it. Even at home I spend all my time on the Internet. Give me a modem and there's no such thing as isolation. I've got the whole world.''

''Maybe so, but this is Wyatt County, where everybody knows everybody else's business, and talks about everything they know.''

''Who cares what they say?'' she asked with false bravado.

''I do. You would. It matters, dammit. I don't want people gossiping about the woman I love. I don't want my sons exposed to that kind of talk.''

''All right.'' Her heart breaking, Belinda closed her eyes and turned away. ''You can call Donna Harris in the morning and hire her, and I'll get out of your way and out of your life so you won't have to listen to any gossip.'' She tried to walk away before he could see the tears threatening to blind her.

He grabbed her arm and stopped her. ''You'd do

that?'' he demanded, incredulous. ''You'd walk out, just walk away, rather than marry me?''

''What do you want me to say?''

''You and I belong together. You can't deny that.''

She would have, but the simple—or not so simple—touch of his hand on her arm, the way her skin responded to his skin, her body to his, would have made a liar out of her. So she said nothing.

''What? Nothing to say?'' He demanded, looking more determined than any man she had ever seen. ''I'll show you just how right we are together.'' With more urgency than finesse, he pulled her to his chest and kissed her, hard and hot and deep.

As it had been that afternoon, so it was now. The explosion of wants, of needs and emotions, came instantly. It was hot and it was powerful.

Belinda knew she should push him away. She couldn't give him what he wanted, couldn't be what he needed. Couldn't marry him. Knowing that for Ace it was all or nothing, marriage or nothing, devastated her, for it meant there was nothing for them. Nothing but this insatiable greed for each other that she felt in her bones and tasted on his lips.

Ace tasted fear on her lips. He hated that, but he understood it. She'd been married before and it hadn't worked out. She'd been disappointed, let down. Trounced on. Now her sister's husband wanted to marry her. Ace knew that in her mind Belinda still compared herself to Cathy and came up wanting.

Damn her for that. If he could, he would kiss that stubborn lack of self-confidence right out of her. He would love it out of her, gentle it out of her.

But just then there wasn't a lot of gentle in him. He'd put everything on the line, his hopes and dreams, his future. His heart and soul. And she'd said no.

Maybe he'd hit her with the idea of marriage too soon. They had only just discovered all these new feelings. At least, he had discovered his. Belinda, he feared, was still denying hers.

She could deny them all she wanted, but they were there. She could be as evasive as hell—and she was. But she loved him. There wasn't a doubt in his mind. She couldn't deny it to herself.

They were in love with each other. It had happened, fast, but they weren't strangers. They knew each other. As far as Ace was concerned, when two people felt this way about each other, they got married.

He supposed he could have been a little more romantic with his proposal, rather than popping the big question at the kitchen sink. But neither one of them was much for fancy trappings or flowery declarations. Maybe she would have appreciated them. More likely she would have laughed in his face.

But she wasn't laughing now, and she was saying no. Yet as he clung to her, desperate to make her see how right they were together, how well they fit, her arms circled his chest and her hands dug into his back as if she never planned to let him go.

He hoped she never let him go, because he didn't intend to let her get away from him. Not in this lifetime. She was his. The taste of her, dark and hot and addictive, was indelibly etched on his taste buds and in his mind. The feel of her pressed against him the way she was now, and when their bodies were more intimately joined, would forever be embedded in his bones. His skin would always know hers. The lure of her, the need, rushed through his blood with every beat of his heart, and always would.

"I want you," he whispered harshly against her lips.

Her response was a tiny whimper of need, a tightening of her arms around his ribs.

"Unless you tell me no," he said, pulling back until he could see her face, "I'm going to carry you upstairs and make love with you."

Belinda struggled to find the will to tell him no, but the word would not come. She wanted him to carry her upstairs, to kiss away all her objections, her fears.

"Ace, I…"

"Are you saying no?"

Tell him, her mind demanded. Making love would solve nothing. She would still be who she was, a woman who felt as if she were stealing her sister's husband, a woman who could never measure up to that perfect, beautiful sister.

"Are you?" he asked again quietly.

"Ace, I…I can't."

He kissed her again, a slow, drugging kiss that melted her willpower. "Can't what, Belinda?" he asked against her lips.

"I can't," she whispered, giving in to her need and his. "Can't say no."

As he swept her up in his arms, Ace's heart raced in relief. He climbed the stairs and carried her to his room.

Without putting her down, he nudged the door closed with his boot and used his shoulder to flip the wall switch that turned on the bedside lamp.

Belinda's gaze locked on the acre of navy comforter on the bed. Her heart started slamming against her ribs. "You expect me to make love with you on Cathy's bed?"

"Slim—"

"I told you not to call me that." With a twist of her body, she slid out of his arms and stood at the foot of the bed. "What am I doing? I'm not— I don't want to be—"

From behind her, Ace slid his arms around her waist and kissed the back of her neck. "You don't want to be what?"

"I don't want to be Cathy." She scrunched her shoulders up and stepped away.

Ace closed his eyes and struggled for the right words. "It's not Cathy's bed, it's mine. Cathy never set eyes on anything in this room. Mary made a lot of changes after Cathy died. I expect you'll want to make a few after we're married."

She whirled on him, fists clenched at her sides. "I told you, I'm not going to marry you. You don't really want me to, and you know it."

"You're wrong," he told her.

The steady look in his eyes nearly crippled her. "You're just lonely, that's all. You think we'll get married and I'll run your house and raise your children the way Cathy did. That I'll play the little woman and wait here at the house and rub your shoulders for you when you come home at night, fetch your pipe and slippers. That I'll be all smiles and kisses, the perfect little earth mother. Well, I won't."

"Believe me, I'm not looking for a mother. I don't own a pipe or slippers. And I'm not looking for another Cathy. I thought we were through with all that."

"How can we be through with it when you bring me to her bed?"

"I brought you to *my* bed!" He closed his eyes a moment, then lowered his voice. "The bed I want to share with you for the rest of my life."

"I can't marry you. Look at me, Ace," she cried. "You call me a nickname that you mean as a compliment, and I go nuts, thinking you're comparing me to Cathy and finding me lacking. You bring me to your room, and I get all upset thinking this is Cathy's bed, that I'm snatching at Cathy's husband, Cathy's children, Cathy's life."

"So you feel guilty for wanting what she had. That doesn't make the wanting wrong. It's the guilt that's wrong, not you or me, or us. We'll work on it. Together."

"This is crazy. I'm crazy. I know that, you know," she admitted, pacing back and forth at the foot of the bed. "I know the envy and the guilt and all of that is crazy. But—" She stopped pacing and looked at him, trying to make him understand. "You're crazy, too, if you think it will all go away because you want it to, and that I'll jump when you snap your fingers."

Ace ground his teeth again, swiftly losing even the desire for patience. "I resent that."

"So do I," she replied hotly.

"I have never snapped my fingers at you or anyone else. I reserve that for the dog."

"Well don't expect my tongue to hang out and my tail to wag if you ever do it to me."

"You're impossible."

"That should tell you we don't belong together."

"It tells me nothing, except that we sure as hell won't be bored for the next fifty or sixty years." He reached for her.

She took a step back, but the bed hit her in the

back of her knees. "We'd probably kill each other before the year was out."

"I'll risk it." He put his hands on her shoulders. "Come here, Slim," he asked softly.

"Please," she begged, fighting her insecurities and losing. "Please don't call me that."

Ace closed his eyes and took a deep breath. "I'm sorry. It's just how I think of you." He looked at her solemnly. "I don't say it to hurt you. I can't believe you're that sensitive, that you can misconstrue something like that."

She hugged herself, unable to meet his gaze.

"All right, let's just take care of this little problem once and for all. Come here." This time he didn't ask. He pulled her gently by the arm and turned until she faced the mirror over his dresser, with him at her back. She started to step away; he wrapped his arms around her and held her against his chest. "Stand still and look, Belinda. Look at yourself and see what I see."

Belinda closed her eyes and turned her head away from the mirror in misery. Why was he doing this to her? He claimed he loved her, yet he was tearing her apart, forcing her to look at her own inadequacies this way. She felt the humiliating sting of tears in her eyes.

"I see a beautiful woman." He spoke softly and placed a kiss on her head.

The kiss was so gentle that the stinging in her eyes grew worse.

"She's got hair the color of midnight, and it's so soft and thick, it makes a man want to sink his fists in it and hold on. When you're outside in the sun there are these incredible highlights, like fire. My mouth goes dry just watching you turn your head in the sunshine.''

Belinda couldn't help it. She opened her eyes. The sight of the two of them in the mirror, with his arms around her, his head above hers, made her throat ache. He couldn't really see her the way he described. He was just trying to make her feel good. This, she supposed, was his sweet side, and it was almost her undoing.

''Your eyes make me want to get lost in them. I never knew how true that old cliché was about being able to drown in a pair of eyes until the first time I saw your eyes go dark with wanting.''

Belinda's heart stumbled.

''When you want me, they're as dark as thunderheads. When you're happy and laughing, they're as light and changeable as morning mist. When you concentrate at the computer they look like new pewter. God—'' he closed his eyes and rubbed his cheek against her hair ''—I love your eyes.''

''Ace...''

''Shh.'' He opened his eyes and met her gaze in the mirror. ''I'm not finished. I haven't told you what your mouth does to me. I don't know if I can. They're so expressive, your mouth and your eyes. If I could drown in your eyes, I want to devour your mouth, with that full lower lip that can pout and smile and tease until I want to beg for mercy. And that's not even considering the way it feels against mine, the way it tastes or what it does to me when you press it against my skin. Just looking at it stirs my blood. You have,'' he said with a smile and a stroke of his forefinger over her lips, ''a beautiful mouth, Slim.''

This time she couldn't work up an ounce of concern over the hated nickname. What did it matter about her body if he thought these things about her mouth, her eyes, her hair? How was it possible to be so thoroughly seduced by words that had little or nothing to do with sex?

"I know." He pulled his arms from around her waist and ran his hands up and down her arms. "I haven't gotten to the crux of the matter, but I will now."

"You don't have to—"

"I do," he countered. "I do have to. I want to." He flashed her a teasing, tender smile. "But I'll apologize in advance if I start drooling on you."

Belinda did not return his smile. She couldn't. She was appalled at how badly she wanted whatever he was about to say to somehow miraculously make her stop comparing herself to Cathy—at least this physical aspect of herself—and come up wanting. She knew she should be able to accept herself for who and what she was without some man—even this man, whom she loved—having to tap dance around her feelings of inadequacy.

"The first thing you have to understand is that I have never—*never*—compared you to Cathy. Not physically, not personality-wise, not in any way. It never occurred to me to compare you. It never occurred to me that anyone would. But you do. That's why I'm doing this, Belinda. Because you keep comparing yourself to her. Being a woman," he said, "I imagine the first thing you'd compare between yourself and Cathy would be these." He cupped his hands around her breasts.

Belinda's various different reactions to what he was doing locked her breath in her throat. First there was the physical pleasure of his touch and the deep need to have him touch her this way. There was the shameful, insecure wish that her breasts were larger so he would like them better—like her better, enjoy her more. *Enjoy her as much as he had Cathy.*

What a bitter emotion. What a bitter feeling in the pit of her stomach to admit such a weakness to herself and know that he knew what she was thinking.

Without her realizing how or when, her blouse was suddenly unbuttoned and his hands were on the bare flesh of her breasts, taking her breath away. "Ace—"

"You're so damn sensitive, so responsive. Look."

The sight of his dark hands against her pale skin made her heart skitter. When he stroked his thumbs over her nipples, she couldn't swallow the moan that rose from deep inside.

"Look," he whispered again. "Look how you respond to my touch. I love touching you like this." His hips nudged against her backside. "Feel what this does to me? And the skin here..." He stroked the underside of one breast. "It's the smoothest skin in the world, soft, like cool silk."

Belinda moaned in protest at the loss of his touch on her nipples.

"I know, I know." He gave her breasts a gentle squeeze. "We're supposed to be talking about size. That's where you've got your sister beat and don't even know it. You're just small enough, barely, to be comfortable without a bra. You can't think for a minute that knowing you never wear one, that you don't need one, doesn't drive me crazy. Me and every other red-blooded man in the world."

With a sweep of his hands, her blouse slid down

her arms. He stepped back enough to let it fall between them to the floor. He stroked her arms, her ribs.

"No," he said, "you can't be considered skinny. There's not a single bone poking through. Just firm, smooth flesh over firm, lean muscle. Feminine muscle that curves and dips right where it should. I wish you could see yourself the way I see you."

Unnerved by his examination of her, she said, "You've made your point." Her voice came out weak and breathless.

"Not yet. If I had, you wouldn't still be feeling uncomfortable standing here like this, looking at yourself, watching me touch you."

"I'm not uncomfortable. It's just—"

"You're fighting the urge to cross your arms over your chest to hide yourself. I don't know which is stronger, wanting to hide from yourself or from me. It hurts me to think of you hiding from yourself, denying yourself the right to look into a mirror and like what you see. It's a different kind of hurt, for me, from when you hide yourself from me. If you could see yourself through my eyes, you'd see a beautiful woman, slender and sexy and beautiful."

Before she realized what he was about to do, he unsnapped her jeans and pushed them and her underwear down to her knees, out of sight in the mirror.

Belinda wanted to protest, but suddenly, incredibly, what she saw in the mirror was not a skinny, shapeless woman. As her gaze followed Ace's hands roaming over her, she saw a lean torso—with no ribs showing as if she didn't get enough to eat. Her waist curved in, then flared out slightly to hips that were narrow, but not too narrow.

"Look at you," he whispered, his hands stroking her hips. "You're slender and shapely and beautiful."

Belinda swallowed a lump of emotion and smiled slightly. "I think the word you're looking for is...slim."

"If you don't like the name, I'll try to quit using it." He smiled back. "But somehow, *slender* just doesn't have the same ring to it."

Quickly he tugged down his own jeans and shorts and kicked them aside. "Look now."

Belinda looked. Her breath caught at the sight in the mirror. She stood slightly before him and to the side. She was fully revealed there, and he was nearly so, with only one arm and the outer edge of his left side hidden by her body.

"Look at us," he urged. He wrapped his left arm around her waist and splayed that hand across her abdomen.

Belinda had never stood this way with a man before. Just stood, and looked. His touch alone would have been enough to make her heart pound, but the sight of them together, him so large, her much smaller, his skin dark, hers pale, his hard muscles, her softer curves...together they were...beautiful.

"What's wrong?" he asked.

Puzzled by the question, she looked into the reflection of his eyes in the mirror. "Nothing. Why?"

"When you look at us in the mirror, you don't see anything wrong?"

There was a trap here, she was sure, but she couldn't see it. Her gaze slid down along their bodies. At the sight of his erection, she swallowed. "No. *Wrong* isn't the word I would use."

"What word would you use?"

Against the back of her shoulder, she felt the strong, steady beat of his heart. "Us. I see us. I don't know what you want me to say."

"Us will do just fine. Because there is an us. You can see it right there. You and me—us. Separately, you're beautiful and I'm not bad." He smiled briefly. "But don't you see? Together we're...perfect. Like two pieces of a puzzle that belong together, that fit together side by side."

"Don't," she beseeched him.

"Don't what? Don't see that we belong together?"

"You're talking about marriage again."

"I'm talking about all of it. Every way we belong together. Every way we match. Our lives, our hearts, our souls." He stroked his hand down her stomach, down lower, until he cupped her between her legs.

Heat pooled. Her bones turned to water. She let out a sharp cry of pleasure.

"Our bodies," he added. Needlessly.

Belinda stared wide-eyed into the mirror, her mind emptied of everything but the sight of their naked bodies, of his hand between her legs. She wasn't a prude, but she felt a little like a voyeur, even if it was herself she was watching. Herself, and Ace.

But the sight did not repulse or appall. It excited. It was the most arousing, erotic thing she'd ever seen. The words he whispered were thrilling, exciting. Loving.

The pounding pleasure built with each flex of his fingers, until she had to bite her lower lip to keep from crying out, from begging him for more.

"Look at me," he whispered.

She barely heard him over the pounding of her own

blood in her ears. She couldn't move, other than
against his hand.

"In the mirror," he said. "Look at me in the mirror. I want to watch your eyes."

"I—can't." But she did it. She met his gaze and
held it while his fingers worked their magic and sent
her higher and higher until she called his name and
shattered.

Watching her was almost more than Ace could
take. Never had he seen anything more arousing than
Belinda's response to him. When her knees buckled,
he gathered her close and took them both down onto
the bed behind him.

He had to have her. Now. But the tears on her face
stopped him. Made his heart stumble. Tenderly, with
a hand that trembled slightly, he brushed the damp-
ness from one cheek. "Belinda?"

She swallowed hard and looked up at him where
he leaned over her. "Oh, Ace, I've never...that
was...incredible."

Ace's heart resumed its heady rhythm. "You're incredible." Tasting her lips, sipping the tears from her
other cheek, he eased himself into the cradle of her
thighs. "Silver," he told her. "When you peak, your
eyes explode from black to silver." Slowly, one inch
at a time, he joined their bodies. "I want to see it
again."

If anyone had asked, Belinda would have told them
she was incapable of responding again just then. But
Ace proved her wrong. The feel of him stretching her,
filling her with his heat and hardness, took her breath
away. Her eyes misted again. Her pulse pounded.
Never did she want this feeling, this closeness with
Ace, to end.

And it didn't end. Ace set the pace, and it was slow and devastating.

Belinda writhed beneath him, reaching for more, for that sharp pinnacle of pleasure she found only with him. Urging him to hurry.

"Easy," he whispered, his voice flowing over her like dark velvet. He pulled almost all the way out, then surged slowly back in, all the way.

The hot, tingling pleasure deep inside her was so exquisite that it bordered on pain.

"We've got all night," he whispered.

Maybe he did, Belinda thought through the fog in her brain, but she was dying. "You're killing me," she protested, her hips rising to meet his next thrust. "I want…"

"What?" His breath was coming harder, faster. "What do you want?"

Gasping, Belinda reached for his shoulders, gratified to feel them slick with sweat. "I want this to never end."

Ace felt his pulse leap at her words. Then she flexed her hips again and he groaned. Soon the pounding, primal rhythm in their blood took over and had its own way with them. The pleasure built until the explosion flashed between them and hurled them over the edge.

It was a long time before either could move again.

And then, without words, they started over.

When the alarm went off at 4:30 the next morning, Ace cursed the presence of mind that had him set it between one long round of lovemaking and the next during the night. If he cared to think about it, which he didn't, he figured they'd had about three hours of sleep.

Still, the morning had its benefits, and they weren't small ones. "Did I ever tell you," he whispered close to her ear, "how much I love waking up with you beside me?"

Belinda sighed. "No, you didn't."

He stroked a hand across her belly. "I love waking up with you beside me."

"You're not so bad to wake up with yourself." She kissed his shoulder. With a stretch and a yawn, she asked, "What was your name again?"

"That's real funny, Slim."

"Ha. If you think that's going to get a rise out of me, forget it. I think I like that nickname now."

Chuckling, Ace wrapped his arms around her and rolled until she lay nestled along his length. "Speaking of somebody getting a rise out of somebody, did I ever tell you what that sexy, morning voice of yours does to me?"

Fully awake now and willing to take advantage of the situation in which she found herself, Belinda wriggled along his body and wrung a moan from him. "I think I get the idea."

It was twenty minutes before Ace dragged her out of bed and into the shower with him. It was another fifteen and an empty hot water tank later before they made it out again.

When she finally headed for the door to go to her room and get dressed, Ace stopped her and gave her a long, slow kiss. Against her lips he whispered, "I love you. Think about me while I'm out mending fence all morning."

As long as they'd been involved in lovemaking,

Belinda had been able to concentrate solely on that, on him. Now he spoke of the day, and work, and unbidden thoughts raced through her mind. Thoughts of his talk of marriage. Thoughts that still terrified her. She turned and opened the door. ''I'll see you at breakfast.''

Chapter Ten

Belinda got off easy at breakfast. When Ace came back from milking the cows, Stoney came with him, so she didn't have to face him alone. And because Ace was in a hurry to get out on the range, he didn't linger after he ate.

"I'll be in for lunch," he told her.

The best she could offer him was a faint "All right."

"We'll talk tonight," he said firmly.

Panic seized her throat and cut off whatever words she might have said as he turned and left the house.

He had not accepted her refusal to marry him. She'd known he hadn't. She was grateful that he hadn't taken their lovemaking to mean she had changed her mind.

Why did he have to go and mess everything up

with talk of marriage? The very idea of getting married turned her blood to ice.

From the day she'd driven up here in her mother's place, Belinda had faced one emotional upheaval after another. She had come here blaming Ace for Cathy's death, only to learn that Cathy's blind, egotistical stubbornness had brought it about. Belinda had been left with an entirely new sense of loss. Cathy may have been dead for two years, but Belinda's memories had been of a perfect, enviable woman, a woman Belinda could never hope to be as good as, as gentle as, as kind as, as beautiful as.

Then all those memories and petty jealousies had been blown to bits by the things Belinda had learned about Cathy, and about herself. About her own feelings for the man who had been her sister's husband.

God, the guilt of wanting him. It had nearly crippled her.

But she'd gotten past that. Mostly. No, not mostly, completely, she realized. She and Ace had a right to be together if they wanted. She knew that, felt it in her heart.

All those traumas had paraded through her life in recent weeks. Not to mention the minor little things like adjusting to life on the ranch, the heavy workload of cooking for a football team. The scare when Grant had been hurt.

Oh, but she did love those boys. If she married Ace—

No. That was a poor reason to marry a man—because you wanted his children.

Ah, now we're getting closer to the heart of the matter, girl.

Yes, the children. Cathy's children, who had no

mother. If any woman had the right to step in and raise those boys, Belinda knew it had to be her. But wouldn't Ace want more children?

Before we were married we knew we wanted four. After Jason, we were hoping for a girl.

At the memory of Ace's words, equal parts of pain and panic seized her. She couldn't do this. She couldn't marry Ace. And because of that, she couldn't stay here on the ranch, taking care of the boys, sneaking into their father's bed late at night. Ace had already said no to that idea. Truth to tell, she feared she would come to hate the sneaking around as much as he would.

"That doesn't leave you many options, does it?" she asked herself.

"What's a opshuns?" Clay asked.

Belinda blinked and focused on the boys eating their breakfast. She hadn't realized she'd spoken aloud. "Options are choices," she explained. "And mine are running out."

"Huh?"

"Never mind." She rose from the table and went to the notepad beside the telephone at the end of the counter. "Hurry up and finish eating, then go make your beds."

"Ah, do we have to?"

"Yes," she said, mimicking the pitiful whine in Jason's voice. "We have to."

The minute they reached the top of the stairs, Belinda reached for the phone. Her hand shook, and her palm was damp. Three times while dialing the number, her stomach clenched painfully. But this was best for everyone. It was the right thing to do. The only thing. She could not face the consequences otherwise.

"Mrs. Harris? This is Belinda Randall at the Flying Ace."

When Ace drove back in for lunch, the first thing he noticed was the gray Oldsmobile parked beside the back door of the house. The same gray Olds that the woman from town had driven when she applied for the job of housekeeper.

Ace's heart stopped. Just flat stopped at the sight of that car.

She wouldn't.

The second thing he noticed was the absence of a certain little red sports car.

He slammed the pickup door and ran.

"Daddy! Daddy!" Jason raced out of the house and down the drive toward Ace. "Daddy, Aunt Binda left!"

Ace skidded to a halt before his son. An invisible vise tightened around his chest. Jason had been crying. "When? Where did she go?"

"She went home. How come she went home, Daddy?" Jason leaned against Ace's legs and sniffed. "We wanted her to stay."

Ace closed his eyes for a second and sought the strength he knew he was going to need. Then he knelt and took his tearful son into his arms. "I know you did, Jason. We all wanted her to stay. Did she say why she…had to leave?"

Jason sniffed again. "No. She just said it was time to go home, and to tell you goodbye."

Equal parts of pain and fury held Ace speechless. Damn her. Damn her to hell for hurting his sons. For tearing his heart out and tossing it away in the dust of her departure. If last night hadn't convinced her how right they were together, Ace didn't know what would. But for her to just up and leave, to walk out like a coward without facing him, that didn't sound like the woman he knew.

So maybe, a voice in his head suggested, *you don't know her as well as you think you do.*

"When's she coming back, Daddy?"

"I don't know, son." *Maybe never. If she can just walk out this way, she might not ever come back.* The thought nearly crippled him. "I don't know."

Jason let out a small sob. "Can we call her and ask her?"

"Sure." But Ace wasn't sure at all. Wasn't sure he could bear to hear the sound of her voice. "After she's had time to get home. Or you could send her an e-mail," he added, hoping the thought of getting on the computer would cheer the boy up.

Jason sniffed again. "Maybe."

"Come on." Ace rose and took Jason by the hand. "Let's go to the house. You can introduce me to our new housekeeper."

Donna Harris took one look at the face of the man before her and knew that her first instinct this morning when she'd arrived at the Flying Ace had been correct—something about this entire situation was not as it should be. The man—Ace Wilder, her boss, she presumed, by the way young Jason clung to his hand—looked positively devastated by her presence in his home.

"Jason," the man said. "Why don't you take your brothers into the living room and watch TV for a few minutes."

"Aw, Dad." Jason looked up at his father and held

on even tighter to the big hand that to him meant safety and security. He didn't want to let go. He wanted Aunt Binda to come back. He wanted his daddy to smile and not look so sad. He didn't want to feel so sad himself.

"Go on, now." His daddy smiled at him, but to Jason it wasn't a real smile. It was one of those smiles grown-ups used when they didn't want you to know something bad was happening. As if a kid couldn't figure it out for himself. Grown-ups could be so dumb sometimes.

"I want to talk to Mrs. Harris," his daddy told him.

Jason sniffed. Crying made his nose all runny. If Aunt Binda was here, she'd give him a tissue and make him blow. "You gonna talk about Aunt Binda?"

His daddy ruffled his hair. "We're gonna talk about scrubbing toilets. You don't want to stick around for that."

Jason frowned. Grown-ups could come up with the dumbest excuses to get rid of kids. But on the outside chance that his daddy and Mrs. Harris really were going to talk about scrubbing toilets, Jason hurried his brothers out of the kitchen. He was just a little kid, after all. Gathering eggs and making his bed and that kind of stuff was okay. But even a little kid had to draw the line somewhere. Jason figured he would draw his at toilets. Aunt Binda wouldn't have made little boys scrub toilets.

Ace watched his eldest son herd his younger brothers down the hall toward the living room. He kept his gaze on the hall until he heard the television come on—anything to postpone the moment when he would have to face the woman in his kitchen.

But now the moment, as well as the woman, was at hand. He turned and faced her. Holding out his hand, he said, "Hi, I'm Ace Wilder."

Donna shook his hand. "Donna Harris. I'm glad to meet you. I assume you weren't expecting me today."

Ace cleared his throat. "Ah, not exactly."

Wondering if she really had this job, Donna offered a nervous smile. "Belinda said she left a note for you in your office. I'll just…get lunch on the table. We can talk after that, if you want."

A note. Relieved, yet sick at heart, Ace gave Mrs. Harris a nod and made his way to his office.

He'd given Belinda his heart. She'd left him with a hand-scribbled sheet of yellow legal paper stuffed inside an envelope with the ranch's return address on it.

"Ace," it said.

Hell. He didn't even rate a *Dear Ace.…*

"I'm sorry. It's cowardly of me, but I couldn't stay."

And that was the sum total of her personal message. Everything else in her note concerned Donna Harris and the arrangements Belinda made with the woman on Ace's behalf. Duties, salary, etc. Not one additional word of a personal nature.

"Damn you, Belinda. Damn you."

Belinda felt damned. Never had she committed such a cowardly act in her life as sneaking away while Ace was gone and leaving his sons with a stranger. He would hate her now.

If it was any comfort to him, she wished he knew how utterly miserable she was. She wished he knew how badly she hurt. How hard it had been to leave him, to leave the boys, the ranch, not knowing if she would ever see any of them again. How empty and barren—*no, don't use that word!*—her apartment felt as she stepped inside late that night and flipped on the light.

The drive had been the longest of her life. Not a mile had gone by that she hadn't remembered one of those three precious faces looking up at her tearfully, asking why she had to leave. She hadn't had the slightest idea how to make them understand a woman's doubts and fears, but she had been determined to put a good face on the situation and not break down and cry with them.

In that, she had failed. When Jason had hugged her legs and said, "But, Aunt Binda, we want you to be our other mother," she'd lost control. She had dropped to her knees and wrapped her arms around all three boys and held them tight, not caring that the new housekeeper could see her silent tears.

Oh, babies, she thought now. *I'm so sorry I made you cry. I miss you so much already. You and your daddy.*

By the time she'd made it twenty miles from the house, she thought she'd had herself under control. Then she remembered little Grant, face red and puffy with tears, patting her on the shoulder and saying,

"Don't cwy, Aunt Binda. We still wuv you."

With that memory, she'd had to pull off the road. There she had buried her face in her hands and let the tears come freely. It took a long time to pull herself together.

And then she'd thought of Ace, and the tears had come again.

Someday, she hoped, Ace would realize that her leaving had been for the best. He would never have been happy married to her. She would have let him down time and time again, in so many, many ways.

As for herself, she would have lived in constant fear of the day he woke and realized that marriage to her was nothing more than a bad joke.

In a stupor of exhaustion and tangled emotions, Belinda left her computer bag on the sofa and staggered toward her bedroom. On the way she paused and looked down at the phone. The message light on her answering machine blinked its little red eye at her.

A shudder of dread made its way down her spine. If she pushed the button, would Ace's voice play back at her?

Maybe in a year or so she would work up the nerve to find out.

Feeling as if the weight of the world were on her shoulders, she turned away, realizing Ace's voice wasn't the only one she had to dread. She would have to call her mother tomorrow and tell her she was home.

No, her mother wouldn't settle for a phone call. If Belinda didn't go in person, her mother would come to her, and Belinda didn't want that. She would have to go herself. She wondered how little she would be able to get away with saying.

At her bedroom door she turned on the light. Her double bed looked small and cold, completely uninviting. Lonely. She would sleep there alone. For the rest of her life.

Suddenly the walls of her small apartment, which she had always considered comfortable and roomy, seemed to close in on her. She tried to shake off the feeling. After all, she had the entire apartment to herself. There was no man to trip over, no little boys to watch out for....

Oh, God, she thought, the pain in her heart nearly stealing her breath.

There was no Ace. No strong arms to hold her in the night, no teasing laughter to lift her spirits. No little carbon copies of him, with their million questions and their heart-stealing smiles. No Jack and Trey—the brothers she'd never had. No Frank or Stoney or Jerry. No goofy dog, no prancing horses, no cows or elk, or moose or coyotes. No wide front porch. No vast, open range to embrace her and soothe her soul.

There was only this small apartment with its thin walls and its emptiness. There would be no soothing of her soul here. This was what she had chosen. She would have to find a way to live with it.

Ace stood on the front porch of his house and looked out across the vast black emptiness that was the range that supported his family. Cool air moved across his skin. Overhead, millions of stars dotted the sky. It was, he supposed, a beautiful night, but he found no pleasure in it.

It was late. Nearly midnight, and he had to get up at four-thirty. It was past the time to go upstairs and face the bed that still smelled of Belinda and their lovemaking.

Had he pushed too hard, too fast? Probably. Obviously. Why else would she have run?

It was plain to him that he'd lost his head. Falling for Belinda had taken him totally by surprise. He hadn't been looking for a woman to fill a void in his life, but when he'd realized he was attracted to her and she to him, that void had opened dark and wide and threatened to swallow him hole. Only Belinda seemed able to save him.

God, he'd fallen fast. And hard. He hadn't known a man could love a woman this way, to the point where he lost all good sense.

Perhaps if he'd kept his head he would have realized that it was more than reluctance to tie herself down that had caused Belinda to refuse his proposal. Only one thing could have sent a tough lady like her sneaking off without a word, and that was terror.

He didn't get it. The Belinda he knew should have stood toe-to-toe with him and argued her point until he saw things her way or convinced her she was wrong. She might have told him bluntly that marriage was a stupid idea and only morons would consider it.

But she hadn't done or said anything like that. She had hired a housekeeper for him without his approval—it was *his* housekeeper, after all; shouldn't he at least have met the woman before she moved into his house? Belinda had packed her belongings, loaded her car, and taken off with nothing more than a scribbled note for the man whose heart she had just ripped to shreds.

"I thought I might find you out here."

At the sound of Jack's voice, Ace heaved a sigh and leaned against the porch post. The same post where Belinda had leaned that first night they'd made love.

Damn, he wished he hadn't remembered that.

"Go away, Jack."

Jack paused in the act of propping a foot on the bottom porch step. Ace was in worse shape than he'd realized. He never told anyone to go away, no matter what. The man was obviously too raw to talk yet.

"All right," he offered quietly. "You wanna talk, you know where to find me."

Ace swallowed. "Thanks. Maybe later."

It went against Jack's nature to let Ace suffer alone. Maybe Ace hadn't welcomed him with open arms that day twenty years ago when Jack's aunt had dropped him at the Flying Ace and left him. But once the two boys had fought things out, they had been there for each other. From the day their father died five years later, they had been more than close. All of them, Trey and Rachel included.

Still, Jack had a deep respect for a man's need for privacy. Sometimes. For now he would leave Ace with his. He said a quiet good-night, then turned and walked back toward his house.

Watching Jack leave, Ace let out a relieved breath. He knew Jack meant well. Jack nearly always meant well, even if Ace didn't always like his brother's methods. But on this night, Ace needed time to himself. To lick his wounds.

Belinda would have postponed letting her parents know she was home, but she was afraid Ace would call them. It didn't seem quite fair for them to find out from him that she was only across town instead of still in Wyoming.

She had spent a miserable night staring with burning eyes at the ceiling over her bed. She'd been afraid to close her eyes, for every time she did, she saw the two of them, Ace and her, reflected in the mirror over his dresser, his hands on her body, making her burn, driving her toward a shattering climax.

That vision was going to drive her insane.

But with her eyes open, her mind was too alert. It

insisted on replaying every moment she'd spent with Ace. Even their arguments made her miss him.

And the boys. Oh, those precious, beautiful boys she'd come to love as her own. She missed them terribly.

Had she made a mistake in leaving? Who would love Ace and hold him through the night, if not her? Who would help him raise his sons?

Some other woman.

She couldn't bear to think about that.

Or maybe no one. Ever again.

That thought, that he might always be alone now, gave her less peace than the thought of him with another woman.

But to give in to him, to marry him...her hands turned to ice at the very idea. Marriage meant being open and honest with each other in all things—at least all things that mattered. It meant adjustments and compromise, and she was lousy at both. It meant putting someone else's needs above her own. She'd never been any good at that, either.

No, she had done the right thing in leaving.

Now, she had to do the right thing and tell her parents she was home. If she didn't give them the gory details, well, a grown daughter had a right to keep some things private from her parents.

Or so she'd always thought. Until she went to her parents' house. The first words out of her mother's mouth, after Belinda told her that Ace had a wonderful new housekeeper who would take good care of the boys, were "What aren't you telling me?"

"I don't know what you mean." Belinda whirled toward the pantry door and opened it. "Got anything to snack on? My cupboards are bare. I didn't have anything for breakfast.''

"Belinda Jean," her mother said in that tone all mothers use now and then to shame their children into confessing something.

"Mom," Belinda said, in that whiny tone all children use to try to avoid answering.

"Come on, dear, sit down at the table. I'll pour you a cup of coffee and scramble you a couple of eggs while you tell me what's wrong.''

"You shouldn't be cooking for me," Belinda protested, grasping at any handy excuse to divert her mother's attention. "You should be—''

"If you use the *R* word on me, so help me, I'll scream.''

"The *R* word?''

"Resting," Elaine enunciated with obvious distaste.

"Oh-ho. Sounds like Daddy's been cracking the whip.''

"He's been treating me like an invalid, is what he's been doing.''

"Mom." Belinda rested a hand lightly on her mother's arm. "You were so sick, you scared us both.''

"I know, honey." Elaine patted her daughter's hand. "I'm sorry you were so worried for me, but I'm fully recovered now. Even your father agrees, and that's saying something. So you sit down and let me mother you with cooking. While you spill the beans," she added sternly.

"Oh, Mama." In defeat, Belinda sank to the chair at the table and buried her face in her hands. "I made such a mess of everything.''

Elaine paused, fighting the urge to take her daughter into her arms and hold her tight. Belinda had not called her Mama more than a handful of times since the age of eight, when she'd decided she was all grown up, and Mama was a baby's word.

Were it Cathy sitting in her kitchen, obviously devastated, Elaine would not have hesitated to offer comfort. But comfort had never comforted Belinda, it only made her feel worse.

Elaine turned toward the refrigerator and took out the package of bacon and the carton of eggs. "What have you made a mess of, honey?"

What the hell, Belinda thought. She scrubbed her hands over her face, then let them fall to the spotless glass tabletop. "It's pathetic, really. And you're not going to like it."

"Do I need to like it?"

"There you go. Why do I always forget how much common sense you have? No, I guess you don't need to like it. But I think it's going to upset you, and I don't want that."

The first strip of bacon started sizzling the minute it hit the skillet. "I have just as much right to get upset now and then as the next person."

"Okay." Belinda took a deep breath and tried to order her thoughts. Maybe if she said it all out loud she could make sense of it. "I discovered something about myself recently that I'm not very proud of."

"That happens to the best of us." When the fourth slice of bacon was in the skillet, Elaine put the package back in the refrigerator. "What did you discover?" she prodded.

In fits and starts Belinda told her. Over scrambled eggs, bacon, toast and her mother's homemade grape jelly, she appalled herself by even admitting that she and Ace had made love.

"Why, the nerve of the man," Elaine stated with a deadpan expression. "Wanting to marry you just because the two of you happen to be in love. How dare the cad."

"But, Mama, I can't marry him, don't you see?"

"No, actually," Elaine said, carrying dirty dishes to the sink. She refilled Belinda's coffee. "I don't see at all, honey."

"Come on, Mom, you know as well as I do that the only reason I married Todd was because he had been Cathy's boyfriend."

"Of course I know it. I wasn't sure that you did."

"How can I ever look myself in the mirror if I turn around and do the same thing again?"

"Belinda," Elaine said, shaking her head, "if you love Ace, and Ace loves you, it shouldn't matter who he was married to before. You've already admitted that you believe you've been attracted to him for years, but it's not like you pushed Cathy off a cliff so you could have him for yourself. Honestly, sometimes I wonder about you, child."

"You don't understand."

"That you've always been envious of Cathy?"

Belinda looked away sharply, ashamed to hear the words from her own mother.

"Of course I understand. And I understand that your father and I contributed greatly to that little problem when you girls were growing up."

Belinda gaped.

"You didn't think we knew what we were doing? Well, we didn't. Not until years later, when the damage was already done. Then we never knew what to do about it, how to correct the situation. You were always so competitive, always wanting to outshine her. And you did, honey, in so many, many ways. In all the important ways, and that pains me on her behalf.''

"I always thought she was so much prettier than I was.''

"She was a very pretty girl, a beautiful woman. So are you.''

"But I'm not blond and curvy. I always thought that if I were, I'd have been as popular as she was, as happy as she was.''

Elaine smiled. "Have you figured out yet that you wouldn't have been?''

"What do you mean? It was all I ever wanted.''

"To be as popular, yes. But you were so busy being envious that I doubt you ever realized that it wasn't Cathy's blond hair and curvy figure that made her so popular.''

Belinda looked up at her mother in disbelief.

"I won't deny they're what got her noticed, but what kept her so popular all her life was that she worked at being popular and well liked. She bent over backward to please everyone around her, to make sure that everyone she came in contact with felt important.''

Belinda's eyes widened as the truth dawned. "She catered to them,'' she said with wonder.

"Of course she did. It's what she loved to do, what she did best.''

"Just like she catered to Ace. I never realized it before.''

"You were too busy wishing you were her. But you would no more have catered to other people's needs than the sun would set in the east, honey, and you know it. You don't have the patience for it."

Belinda gave her mother a wry grin. "You could have saved me a lifetime of grief if you had pointed this out years ago."

Elaine chuckled. "I pointed it out a dozen times when you were in high school, sweetheart. You didn't believe me. You thought if you bleached your hair, that would take care of it."

A burst of startled laughter escaped Belinda. "I remember that. Oh, God, what an idiot I've been."

"So, now that you've realized all of this, where does that leave you with Ace? You really shouldn't punish the poor man, or deny yourself, just because he was married to your sister."

"Oh, Mama." Belinda sighed. "It's not that. I was dealing with that part of it. It's just…we're so different, Ace and I."

"I don't think that's what you mean."

"No, you're right. I keep thinking he will expect me to be the happy little homemaker, like Cathy was. I don't mean that in a bad way about Cathy. She was so good at making a home for him and the boys, taking care of them."

"Catering to them?"

"Yes. And I know Ace realizes I'm not like her. But I don't think he understands how really different being married to me would be. I don't think he'd like it. I'm not sure I would. If he started expecting too many concessions on my part, I'm sure I wouldn't."

Elaine took a sip of coffee.

When she didn't comment, Belinda shifted restlessly in her chair. "What?" she asked. "Nothing to say?"

Elaine smiled slightly. "I'm sure I'll have more to say when you get to the real reason you tucked your tail between your legs and ran home. Not that I'm not glad to have you, dear," she added with a pat on Belinda's hand. "But nothing you've told me so far seems insurmountable."

"Your sympathy," Belinda said darkly, "overwhelms me." When her mother merely sat there and looked at her, Belinda closed her eyes. "All right." She couldn't say this while looking at anyone. Could barely say it at all. The only way she could do it was to get the words out in one long rush. "He doesn't know a certain fact about me that a prospective husband should know about the woman he thinks he wants to marry."

When her mother still remained silent, Belinda finally opened her eyes and looked at her. "There. I said it. Are you satisfied now?" The sympathy on her mother's face was almost her undoing.

"Oh, honey." Elaine's lips wobbled. "Don't you see? You still haven't said it. You've never said the words out loud, have you?"

Chapter Eleven

Ace had hoped that after a few days, the boys would become accustomed to Belinda's absence and stop asking him when she was coming back.

It wasn't happening. He didn't know why he thought it would. *He* hadn't grown accustomed. *He* hadn't stopped asking. But for him there was no one to ask. Unless, of course, he wanted to ask the woman herself.

What a little sneak she'd turned into, he thought, grinding another layer of enamel off his teeth in sheer frustration. She had called the boys the day after she left—in the middle of the afternoon, when she knew he wouldn't be anywhere near the house— and talked to them for, according to Jason, hours. Mrs. Harris allowed that all three boys had talked on the phone and hung up in less than ten minutes.

"Do you think she'll come back tomorrow?" Jason

asked as Ace tucked the boys in for the night. Funny how quickly Ace had gotten used to Belinda being there with him for the nightly ritual. Four nights after she'd gone, and he still expected to find her there when he turned.

"What's the matter?" Ace asked, grateful that the question was accompanied by only a slight sniff rather than the heartbreaking sobs from earlier in the week. Grateful, too, that Clay and Grant had elected Jason as their spokesperson on the subject of Belinda, so that Ace only had to face the questions from his eldest rather than all three of them. "I thought you liked Mrs. Harris."

Dangling one leg off the upper bunk, Jason shrugged. "She's okay. She cooks better than Aunt Binda."

Ace couldn't help but grin at the comment. For a six-year-old to notice such a thing, either Belinda's cooking had been worse than Ace had realized, or Mrs. Harris's was better than he'd noticed.

"But she won't come outside and have squirt-gun fights or nothin'. An' she can't make a spit ball or a paper airplane."

"She can't, huh?" Ace seemed to recall that the woman had raised four younger brothers. "Did you ask her?"

"We-ell, not exactly."

"She might surprise you if you give her a chance."

"Okay," Jason said, his lower lip wobbling. "But we sorta thought maybe Aunt Binda would be our new mom."

Ace felt like he'd been kicked in the gut. He had to wait until his hand stopped trembling before he reached up and tucked the dangling leg beneath the covers. "I, uh, didn't know you wanted a new mom."

"Well, heck, yeah, Dad," Jason said matter-of-factly, his threatening tears drying up. "A guy needs a mom, doesn't he? I mean, who's gonna make sure we don't spit in public, and all that other stuff?"

Ace gave the boy a mock frown. "I am, buster, and don't you forget it." He ran his fingers over Jason's ribs with deliberate intent.

Extremely ticklish, Jason screamed with laughter. Nothing else would do, then, but for Clay and Grant to climb out of bed with the weak—and very false—excuse of coming to their brother's aid. Ace obliged them all by dragging Jason from the top bunk so that the four of them could roll on the floor together while they all tickled each other.

From the doorway Jack and Trey shook their heads, while Donna Harris smiled.

"I told you they weren't killing each other," Trey said smugly to Jack.

"You did not."

"Unca Trey, Unca Jack," Clay shrieked with laughter. "Help us! He's tryin' to tickle us to death."

"Not me," both men said at once.

"Maybe Mrs. H. will help," Trey offered.

"Oh, no." Donna Harris backed away from the door. "Besides, it looks to me like they've got him under control."

"Buried is more like it," Jack offered cheerfully, seeing the three youngsters pile on top of their father.

After a couple of minutes Ace let out a loud roar that sounded like a charging lion, and little boys tumbled to the floor amid more shrieks of laughter.

"Lordy," Ace complained, gasping for breath and

hugging his side where someone's foot had connected. "I'm getting too old for this. You boys 'bout did the ol' man in that time."

It took nearly fifteen minutes to get the boys settled down in bed again, but Ace didn't regret it. It seemed like he never got to spend as much time with them as he wanted anymore.

When the adults left them and went downstairs, Donna told the men good-night and retired to her room off the kitchen.

"What brings you two here?" Ace asked, offering each of them a beer.

Trey rubbed the side of his nose. He glanced quickly at Jack, then looked back to Ace. "How about poker?"

"Poker?" Ace arched a brow.

"You haven't been down to the bunkhouse for a game in months." Trey pulled a worn deck of cards from his hip pocket.

With a shrug, Ace headed for the kitchen table. He didn't believe for a minute that poker was why they'd come, but what the hell. "Why not? Sounds good." Anything to occupy his mind and keep him from brooding about Belinda sounded good to Ace. He grabbed the deck out of Trey's hands. "My deal."

"Hey, wait a minute," Trey protested. "It's my deck."

"It's my table."

"Now, boys." Jack snatched the deck from Ace. "If we're not going to play nice—"

It had been years since the three of them had engaged in a wrestling match. They had outgrown the need to test each other long ago. But as one, as if on cue, Ace and Trey pounced on Jack. Just for the hell of it.

Behind the closed door to her bedroom off the kitchen, Donna heard a shout, a thud, a chair crashing to the floor. She put down the novel she'd been reading, threw open her door, then shook her head. Little boys upstairs, big boys downstairs.

Suddenly she smiled. She was going to feel right at home in this house, yes, she was. "You break anything, you clean it up," she called before closing her door and settling down again with her book. Yes, sir, right at home indeed.

Out in the kitchen, Ace rolled off Jack and sat up. "That's the trouble with having a woman in the house."

"Yeah," Trey allowed, with a grimace toward the housekeeper's door. "They take all the fun out of everything."

Jack grunted and climbed to his feet. "I'm glad you thought that was fun."

Ace joined him and retrieved his beer from the counter beside the refrigerator. "You're just ticked because we ganged up on you."

Jack grabbed his own beer and slugged down half of it in two long gulps. "Why would that tick me off? The day I can't take both of you is the day I hang up my spurs."

"If I wasn't so tired," Ace said, "I'd make you prove that. Where's the cards?"

Trey snorted. "Look around, big brother. They're everywhere."

They were, indeed. Scattered all over the kitchen floor, with the six of clubs in the sink.

"Well, hell, Trey," Ace told him. "Poker was your idea. Pick 'em up."

Trey started to protest, but at a look from Jack, he thought better of it and gathered the cards.

Interesting, Ace thought, seeing the look pass between his brothers.

Without words, the three men took their places at the kitchen table. Ace grabbed the deck from Trey. "My deal."

Trey pursed his lips. "I bow to your age, old man. Go ahead."

"Dealer's choice. Five-card stud." Ace began to shuffle. "I hope you boys brought money. Whatever you really came here for, this is gonna cost you." He raised one hip and pulled out his wallet. "Ante up, boys."

"What is it you think we came here for?" Trey asked as he and Jack pulled out their own wallets.

After they each tossed a five-dollar bill to the center of the table, Ace dealt each man one facedown hole card. "You want to pick this thing to pieces, dissect it, analyze all the angles. You always do."

"Do we?" Trey asked.

"Jack does." Ace peeked at his hole card, then dealt each man a second card, this one faceup. He noted irritably that neither Trey nor Jack bothered to ask which "thing" he thought they wanted to pick to pieces. "Jack figures all the angles first before he acts. Hell, he probably plans out his whole damn day before he gets out of bed every morning."

"Think you know me that well, do you?" Jack asked casually.

"I think my ace is high, so it's my bet." Ace tossed

a ten into the pot. "And yeah, I guess I know you that well."

"Good." Seated to Ace's left, Jack looked at his own hole card, then tossed in a ten-dollar bill to stay in the game. "Then you already know what I came to say, so I don't have to say it."

Ace snorted. "You're going to say I blew it. Big-time."

"Well," Trey said laconically as he tossed in his own ten, "there is that."

"Gee," Ace said, "I never would have figured it out on my own. Thanks, fellas, for telling me."

This time it was Jack who snorted. "Way I figure it, Belinda's the one who blew it. She fits here. She likes it here. And any fool could see how crazy she was about you."

Ace felt his heart clench. "Oh, yeah, she was real crazy about me, all right." He dealt each man a second faceup card. "So crazy that the thought of marrying me sent her running out of here so fast it'll take another week for her dust to settle."

It was quiet for a minute while they studied their own cards and each other's. The pair of fours that Jack had faceup was the highest combination so far, so it was his bet.

"Marriage, huh?" Jack finally said, tossing another ten into the pot. "So that's what did it."

"Funny," Trey said. "I'll see your ten and raise you five more. I never figured the fox for a quitter."

"Me, neither," Ace admitted. He met Trey's fifteen-dollar bet, then picked up the remainder of the deck and dealt them each a third faceup card. "Did you think it was you?" he asked Jack. "Your little stunt of dragging us out to the cemetery that sent her running?''

Taking another look at his hole card, Jack shrugged. ''Thought it might be possible.''

''Forget that,'' Ace told him. ''Actually, that turned out to be a good thing. Not that I much care for the way you went about it.''

''My pair of tens beats anything showing.'' Since that made it his bet, Jack threw another ten in the pot. ''I won't apologize for it.''

''What, your pair of tens?''

''The trip to the cemetery. I know I was sticking my nose in, but it looked to me like you both needed your eyes opened.''

''Or your butts kicked,'' Trey added as he met Jack's bet.

''You're all heart, you two.'' Ace placed his bet and dealt the fourth and final faceup card.

''Yeah.'' Jack arched his back and stretched his arms over his head. ''That's what I hear.'' After another minute of quiet while they studied the cards he said, ''So, what are you gonna do?''

Now that, Ace thought to himself, was the question of the hour. Of the decade. A dozen scenarios had been running through his mind since it had cleared enough to let him think.

''What I'd really like to do,'' he admitted, ''is get drunk.''

''That'll show her,'' Trey said with a snicker.

''But instead, since I've now got a pair of aces showing, I'll bet twenty dollars.''

''But what,'' Jack prodded, ''are you going to do about Belinda?''

''I'm not going to do anything,'' Ace finally said.

"What? You screw up so bad that she runs all the way home, and you're not going to try to fix it?" Jack demanded.

"Fix it?" Ace cried. "What makes you think her leaving was my fault?"

"Brother, brother," Jack said, shaking his head. "What are we going to do with you? There's not a person alive who couldn't watch the two of you together and see how much Belinda loves you. It's damn awe inspiring is what it is. She's not a quitter, and she's not a runner. She's a fighter. Whatever you did must have been pretty bad to make her run out like that."

"Your faith in me warms my heart, bro." But Ace had to figure Jack had a point. Talk of marriage. That's what had sent Belinda running. "Are you gonna bet or fold?"

"Neither until you swear you're going to fix it with you and Belinda."

"I don't think I can fix it," Ace confessed. "She's dead-set against marrying me."

"Maybe she's gun-shy," Trey offered. "Being divorced and all."

"That's part of it."

"Did she tell you the rest? I'm not asking you to tell me," Jack said quickly. "The details are none of my business."

Ace whooped. "This, from the man who lectured both of us out at Cathy's grave?"

"Hey, a man can only watch you two flounder for so long without having to take matters into his own hands. I'm just asking if you know why she wouldn't marry you. Seemed like the next logical step to me."

"It did to me, too," Ace admitted. "She didn't see it that way."

"She still thinking she's snatching at her sister's husband?"

Ace shrugged. "Who knows what she thinks? Who knows what any woman thinks?"

Trey snorted. "You got that right."

"She just couldn't see it," Ace confessed morosely.

"Couldn't see what?" Jack asked.

"How right we are together. I tried to show her, but…"

Jack snorted. "With a woman like her, you'd probably have been better off *daring* her to marry you instead of asking her. You know she can't resist a challenge."

Ace would have bet that nothing could make him laugh, but he found himself chuckling at Jack's suggestion. "I can't wait till *you* fall. I wanna be there to see you dare some woman to marry you. And here I thought you were on my side."

"Hey, I'm on my side. The happier you are, the easier you are to get along with."

"See my bet or fold, Jack."

"I still say sweet talk won't do it with Belinda. She's too damn contrary."

"You want me to marry a contrary woman?"

"She'll keep you on your toes."

"She's gone, Jack."

"Maybe you should have told her you wouldn't marry her if she begged you."

"Yeah, right," Ace muttered. "You gonna finish this hand, or you wanna open up the new hot line— Jack's Advice to the Lovelorn?"

Trey whooped with laughter.

Jack sneered. Then, with a curse, he folded.

Trey's laughter trailed off as his brothers stared at him. All he had to beat was a pair of aces. "Hell. I fold."

Well, Ace thought after his brothers left, at least he hadn't lost his luck with cards. But he wished they had stuck to playing poker instead of talking. Talking about Belinda just made him think about her that much more, miss her that much more. Made him pull out, one more time, each minute they'd spent with each other. He searched his memory for every word, every smile, every cocky smirk she'd given him.

By morning he decided he'd had enough. She loved him. He knew she loved him. How dare she walk away and leave him in pieces this way?

Hell, whose damn fool idea was it for him to fall in love again, anyway? The last time around hadn't been nearly this painful. Hadn't been painful at all, as a matter of fact. Until the end, when it had nearly killed him.

He couldn't believe he'd come this close to complete happiness again, only to have it end this way. Not as devastating as watching Cathy die in his arms, to be sure. But that had been out of his control. This didn't have to be.

Belinda Randall was not going to get away with this.

Every Sunday afternoon since Belinda had left her parents' nest, she had gone to their house for dinner. Her first Sunday home from Wyoming was no exception. Her father grilled steaks on the patio, and afterward, when the kitchen was cleaned up, the three of them sat around the den, which overlooked the patio at the back of the house, complaining about having overeaten.

"It was the brownies and ice cream that did it," Belinda moaned as she lounged in her father's recliner while he lay on the couch with his head in Elaine's lap, acting as if he were dying.

"The bread," he said with a pitiful groan. "Too much French bread."

"You're both right," Elaine proclaimed. "We'll never have either again."

"Now, Mother," Howard said cautiously. "Let's don't make any hasty decisions. We might recover, you know."

"You might," Belinda claimed. "I'm done for. You'll need a wheelbarrow to get me out of here."

The doorbell rang.

Howard groaned again. "Who would dare?"

"You poor thing." Elaine patted his shoulder and slid out from beneath his head. "I'll get it."

When she left the room, Belinda smiled at her father. "I'm proud of you, Daddy."

"Why, thanks. I'm proud of you, too. What are you proud of me for?"

Belinda chuckled. "You let her walk all the way to the front door by herself."

Howard grimaced. "I'm trying."

"And you're doing very well."

"It's no secret that she scared the dickens out of me with that pneumonia," he said, pushing himself up until he sat upright on the couch.

"I know." Belinda swallowed at the memory of how sick her mother had been. "She scared me, too.

If you hadn't been here to take care of her, I never could have gone to Wyoming.''

''I hear voices,'' he warned. ''Sounds like we've got company.''

Assuming it was a neighbor, Belinda lowered the footrest of the recliner and raised the back until she could sit up straight.

Elaine burst into the room. ''Look who's here!''

Belinda turned toward the door with a smile of greeting—and froze. ''Ace.'' By some miracle of physiology, her heart jumped up into her throat and started quivering. Belinda bolted from the chair and stood, hands clenched at her sides, wishing she could run and hide, but knowing her feet were nailed to the floor. Oh, God. What was he doing here? Why had he come?

She nearly ate him alive with her eyes, but she couldn't help it. He was the absolute last person she ever expected to see anytime in the near future. But there he stood, big and bold as life—bigger. Bolder. He looked so good, she wanted to weep.

But he looked tired, too, as though he hadn't been sleeping. Belinda tried not to be thrilled by that, but her heart gave a little leap, anyway.

''Howard.'' With his gaze locked on Belinda, Ace greeted her father. He transferred his white Stetson to his left hand and shook hands with Howard.

The tension in the room was palpable. No one spoke. No one, it seemed, breathed.

Then Ace took a single step toward Belinda. ''Look me in the eye,'' he demanded, ''and tell me you don't love me.''

Howard jerked once, then stilled.

Elaine quietly held her breath.

Belinda sucked hers in. She opened her mouth to speak, to deny the statement, but the lie wouldn't come.

Ace gave a sharp nod. "That's what I thought." He took another step and reached for her.

Belinda panicked. "I can't have children," she blurted. An instant later heat flamed across her face. She could have bitten her tongue off.

Slowly Ace lowered his hand to his side. "What?"

Belinda squeezed her eyes shut. "God, don't ask me to say it again."

"Slim, I...I didn't know. Does it have to do with your miscarriage?"

Stricken, Belinda opened her eyes and looked at him. "You know about that?"

He gave her a half smile. "You know Cathy couldn't keep a secret. Not usually, anyway," he amended. They both knew he was referring to her keeping her own pregnancy a secret from him that last time.

"Well, then," Belinda managed. "Now you know the truth."

"Okay." When she didn't say anything else, he frowned. "I don't mean to make light of the fact that you can't have children, but—what does that have to do with whether or not you love me?"

"Ace," she cried, gaping at him. "Pay attention here. You didn't know about this when you asked me to marry you."

"What? You think this makes a difference to me? For your sake, I'm sorry you can't have children. But hell, Slim, after what happened to Cathy, do you think I could actually survive another pregnancy by a woman I love? If children are important to you, I've got three who took a vote and decided they wanted you for their new mom. They may not be of your body, but aren't they the next best thing?''

Staggered, Belinda placed a hand over her chest to keep her heart from pounding its way out. "I don't believe this. The man who breeds things for a living, who always said he wanted four children, doesn't care that the woman he's asked to marry him can't get pregnant? You can't be serious.''

"I've never been more serious. I love you. You love me. I want to spend the rest of my life with you.''

"Yeah, well, that's what my ex said, too.''

"Yeah, well,'' Ace said, "take a good look, Slim. I'm not your ex. When you figure that out and decide you want to marry me, you know where to find me. The next move is yours.''

Then, incredibly, he turned away and said goodbye to her parents. Then he walked straight out of the house. A second later she heard the sound of an engine revving, then fading away down the street.

"Well,'' Elaine said, letting out her breath.

Howard looked from his wife to his daughter and back again. "I guess maybe there's a little something the two of you haven't told me?''

"He left,'' Belinda said, stunned. "He came all the way to Denver, stayed five minutes, then…just left.''

"Looks that way,'' Howard said, stuffing his hands into the front pockets of his slacks.

Something inside Belinda, something that had been frozen for days, broke free. Suddenly her vision cleared, as if a fog had just lifted. The world had been off kilter, but was now back on its axis the way it should be.

And she was furious. "How dare that rotten, hayseed cowboy come here this way and get me all stirred up again, get me to admit my darkest secret—" The secret that for years had nearly crippled her, that, until Ace, had made her feel less than a whole woman "—then just walk out? How *dare* he."

"Hmm. Yes," Elaine murmured. "Indeed."

"If he thinks I'm going to let him get away with this, he's dead wrong, oh, yes, he is."

"Whatever you say, honey."

Looking lost and confused, Howard flopped back down onto the couch. "I'd just be happy if somebody would tell me what the dickens was going on and why I've been kept in the dark."

Almost as fast as it had come, Belinda's anger drained away. She stood there in the middle of the room suddenly feeling as lost and confused as her father looked. "What am I going to do?"

"Do you really love him?" her mother asked quietly.

"More than anything," Belinda answered with all her heart. "More than anything."

It was barely a hundred miles up I-25 from Denver to Cheyenne. Ace knew, because he counted every one of them as he kept one eye on the traffic and the other on the rearview mirror. She would have to go home and pack, he told himself. That's why she hadn't caught up with him yet. She just hadn't had time.

From Cheyenne across I-80 to the state highway that cut through Wyatt County, it was three hundred and fifty miles. He kept his speed down to seventy to give her a chance, but five hours after leaving Cheyenne, when he turned off I-80 for the last hundred-mile stretch, there was still no little red sports car riding his tail.

She was trying to scare him, that was it. She was going to let him stew all the way home, then she'd show up tomorrow and give him holy hell.

But tomorrow came, and Belinda didn't. Neither did she come, or call, the next day, nor the day after that. Each day, Ace found it harder to keep his hope alive that she would come back to him.

It was four days before he admitted to himself that she wasn't coming. He'd blown it. He shouldn't have driven all the way down there with a chip on his shoulder. He shouldn't have put her on the spot like he had. And in front of her parents.

He shouldn't have walked away from her.

He should have asked her to sit and talk with him. He should have asked her to please come home with him, please marry him. He should have gone down on his knees and begged, if that's what it took to get her back. Offered to live with her if she wouldn't marry him.

Maybe he should call her. He gave his horse a final pat and turned him out into the corral. Hoisting the saddle, blanket and bridle over his shoulder, he turned toward the barn, figuring he would have to wait until the boys were in bed tonight before he would have the privacy to make the call.

From the corner of his eye, he saw a rooster tail of dust shooting up off the road from the highway. As the dust shot closer toward the house, he mentally tallied the location of everyone on the ranch and knew they were all here. This wasn't someone returning home.

He couldn't make out the vehicle, but it was too small to be a pickup, even one of those little jobs.

Slowly, with his heart speeding up, he eased the saddle and gear back onto the top rail of the corral.

He was too relieved to grin when he made out the little red sports car, but it was tempting. So was throwing his hat in the air and letting out a whoop of sheer joy at seeing his future speed up that damned ol' dirt road.

She didn't stop at the house, but barreled straight for him so fast that for a minute he thought she planned to run him down. He'd be damned before he would back up. A smart man didn't show fear in front of this woman.

Behind him he heard several of the men coming out of the barn. He ignored them and kept his eyes on the car.

At the last possible second, she slammed on the brakes. The car skidded sideways to a halt six feet from the toes of his boots and sent a cloud of dust boiling into the air. When the dust cleared, she opened the door, climbed out and marched around to stand at the front of the growling little vehicle.

Tension coiled in Ace's belly. "Tell me you're not lost," he said tightly. "Tell me you came here on purpose."

She didn't want him to see her wipe her nerve-dampened palms on her jeans, so Belinda stuffed her hands into her back pockets. She tried for a casual pose, but inside she was quaking. "I came here on purpose," she stated.

"Thank God," Ace whispered.

When he held out his arms, Belinda let out a glad cry and gratefully fell into them. He hugged her so hard she thought her ribs might crack, but she didn't care. Never had anything felt so right as being wrapped in Ace Wilder's embrace. Finally, Belinda was exactly where she belonged.

He kissed her ear, her neck. "I was afraid you weren't coming."

"I couldn't stay away," she whispered. "You knew I couldn't. Kiss me, Ace. Kiss me."

Ace didn't need a second invitation. He took her mouth greedily, starved for the taste of her. Footsteps crunched on gravel. He barely heard them, easily ignored them. He could have ignored an earthquake just then, as long as Belinda went on kissing him.

He had questions. Dozens of them, that he was almost afraid to ask. But as his initial hunger was assuaged and the kiss turned gentle, he knew he had to ask. "Are you staying? Tell me you're staying."

Belinda pulled back slightly and met his gaze. With a slightly wobbly smile, she said, "I guess I'll have to. I put all my belongings in storage and vacated my apartment. I, uh, understand you have an opening here."

Ace eyed her carefully. "You want to be my housekeeper?" he asked warily.

Belinda arched a brow. "Me? You must be joking. I know for a fact that you already have a housekeeper, and if I have anything to say about it, she'll be staying. I was talking about the position as wife to one Ace Wilder."

His smile came slowly and made her heart race. "Oh, yeah? You're gonna marry me?"

"Oh, cowboy." She tugged his hat off and tossed it over her shoulder onto the hood of her car, then wrapped her arms around his neck and pulled him close again. "Am I ever gonna marry you."

It was the nearby voices that broke their heated kiss.

"What do you think, Number Three?" Jack said.

Trey chuckled. "I think it's about damn time."

"Ah," Belinda said to Ace. "That would be the prospective brothers-in-law."

Up the driveway, the back door of the house slammed, and childish shrieks split the air. "It's Aunt Binda! Aunt Binda's back!"

"And that," Ace told her, smiling warmly, "would be the prospective sons."

Belinda stepped from Ace's embrace and turned in time to kneel in the gravel and catch the three little bodies who launched themselves at her. As she hugged Jason, Clay, and Grant to her chest, her vision blurred. She had everything now. The man she loved, two new brothers, a new sister off at college and the children of her heart.

A soft feeling of warmth swept over like a summer breeze, and suddenly Belinda knew that Cathy, wherever she was, was smiling.

* * * * *

*Meet Ace, Jack and Trey's younger sister,
Rachel Wilder, when her former love,
Grady Lewis, comes home to Wyatt County.
Coming to Special Edition in the
spring of 2000.*

THE FORTUNES OF TEXAS

*Membership in this family has its privileges
…and its price.
But what a fortune can't buy,
a true-bred Texas love is sure to bring!*

Coming in October 1999…

The Baby Pursuit

by

LAURIE PAIGE

When the newest Fortune heir was kidnapped, the
prominent family turned to Devin Kincaid to find the
missing baby. The dedicated FBI agent never expected
his investigation might lead him to the altar with
society princess Vanessa Fortune.…

THE FORTUNES OF TEXAS continues with
Expecting… In Texas by **Marie Ferrarella**,
available in November 1999 from
Silhouette Books.

Available at your favorite retail outlet.

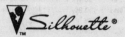

Silhouette®

SILHOUETTE BOOKS
is proud to announce the arrival of

THE BABY OF THE MONTH CLUB:

the latest installment of author
Marie Ferrarella's
popular miniseries.

When pregnant Juliette St. Claire met Gabriel Saldana than she discovered he wasn't the struggling artist he claimed to be. An undercover agent, Gabriel had been sent to Juliette's gallery to nab his prime suspect: Juliette herself. But when he discovered her innocence, would he win back Juliette's heart and convince her that he was the daddy her baby needed?

Don't miss Juliette's induction into
THE BABY OF THE MONTH CLUB
in September 1999.
Available at your favorite retail outlet.

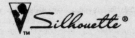

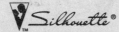

Sometimes families are made in the most unexpected ways!

Don't miss this heartwarming new series from
Silhouette Special Edition®, Silhouette Romance®
and popular author
DIANA WHITNEY

Every time matchmaking lawyer
Clementine Allister St. Ives brings a couple
together, it's for the children...
and sure to bring romance!

August 1999
I NOW PRONOUNCE YOU MOM & DAD
Silhouette Special Edition #1261
Ex-lovers Powell Greer and Lydia Farnsworth knew *nothing*
about babies, but Clementine said they needed to learn—fast!

September 1999
A DAD OF HIS OWN
Silhouette Romance #1392
When Clementine helped little Bobby find his father, Nick Purcell
appeared on the doorstep. Trouble was, Nick wasn't Bobby's dad!

October 1999
THE FATHERHOOD FACTOR ·
Silhouette Special Edition #1276
Deirdre O'Connor's temporary assignment from Clementine
involved her handsome new neighbor, Ethan Devlin—and
adorable twin toddlers!

Available at your favorite retail outlet.

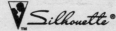

Coming this September 1999
from SILHOUETTE BOOKS
and bestselling author

RACHEL LEE

CONARD COUNTY:
Boots & Badges

Alicia Dreyfus—a desperate woman on the run—
is about to discover that she *can* come home
again…to Conard County. Along the way she
meets the man of her dreams—and brings together
three other couples, whose love blossoms beneath
the bold Wyoming sky.

Enjoy four complete, **brand-new** stories in one
extraordinary volume.

Available at your favorite retail outlet.

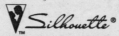